URN

YOUR

KEEP

PERSEPHONE PRINGLE COZY MYSTERIES: TWO

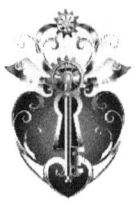

PATTI LARSEN

ISBN: 978-1-989925-77-5

CHAPTER ONE

I closed the filing cabinet drawer, turning to my therapy partner who observed from her patient place on the hardwood floor, staring up at me with those brilliant green eyes observing with her usual feline mix of judgment and adoration. While we'd only been our own little family for four months now, Belladonna's presence felt as comfortable as if we'd known one another forever.

Yes, I was talking about a cat. For whatever reason, this particular white floof with her pink nose and giant tail that covered her paws in a fluffy shroud while she stared with that intense emerald gaze had filled a hole in my life I didn't even know existed until she adopted me.

"Want dinner, sweet girl?" She chirped in response, her vocal range quite impressive, as was her penchant for assisting in my therapy sessions. As I followed her, Belladonna's tail in a soft question mark, sashaying her elegant way through my office door to the hall, I still marveled at how the cat her previous owner said didn't like anyone had become a constant companion for me and those who wished for her comfort during their time with us. From the very first day I'd had her home she'd made herself a part of my life as easily as if she'd been born here instead of a few hours away. Not to mention pawing her way into the office and jumping into assorted laps of various clients who instantly loved her and hugged her and used her as support while they unraveled their troubles.

Who knew? Aside from one or two allergic individuals I had to lock her away from, Belladonna's presence enhanced my own techniques in ways that felt as natural and right as the tools I used to help those who came to me for aid.

Bringing her home had been the right choice and a happy ending to a sad beginning for her and a frustrating one for me. Never mind she saved my life not so long ago, either. Despite my years without a pet thanks to my ex-husband's own reactions requiring tons of medication, I was now the proud human of the best kitty ever. We made a great team.

I closed the door to the office area of the house, passing the front door to the kitchen, Belladonna's practiced path to her food bowl as common now as my own.

"Chicken or salmon tonight?" She meowed her answer, rubbing against my leg while I dished out a half can of lean pink fish for her to enjoy, bending to scratch her cheek. "You did wonderfully today, you know." I had no illusions I was turning into a crazy cat lady, divorced at fifty and already with my starter kit waiting for her dinner at my feet. "Thank you for your help, my darling." The moment the dish hit the floor I no longer existed, though she did glance up, purring as she ate, eyes blinking a dreamy blink before she dove back into her meal.

I didn't get a chance to make my own, the sound of voices following the opening and closing of the front door, my daughter, Calliope, and her best friend Thalia making themselves at home as much as Belladonna had. Not that I minded, a hug from both ending my day in the best way possible, keys supplied to my kid the day I moved in for just that reason.

I might have moved across town from her father and our old house, but this would always be her home, too.

"Mom, Thalia needs a favor from you." My daughter's round cheeks were already pink with emotion, her initial tell she was worked up about something impossible for her to hide. Not to mention the fact she'd skipped the usual *how was your day* preamble for a deep dive into the issue at hand.

Well, I'd raised her, to be honest.

"Anything, you know that." I leaned against the counter with one hip. "Would you two like to discuss said favor over dinner?"

The girls exchanged a look, the radical difference in the two doing nothing to eliminate the clear connection between them. Thalia's tall, almost willowy body showed barely a curve despite her twenty-one years, near androgynous shape paired with the palest pin-straight blonde hair and blue eyes, porcelain skin really needing a little sunlight though I knew she burned at the drop of a hat. My daughter, for her part, inherited her father's shorter, stouter figure, athletic as opposed to slim, brown curls as unruly as ever despite her attempts to tame them, hazel eyes large on her freckled face.

"Thank you, Seph," Thalia said in her light, quiet voice, smiling at me with enough sadness behind it I knew something big was up. "That would be lovely."

Callie seemed to hesitate before shrugging, slipping out of her denim jacket. "Dinner it is," she said while sounding like impatience had a hold of her and wasn't going to back down anytime soon.

"How about I cook and you two talk," I said. "What's up?"

Thalia hesitated, as if unable to say what she wanted to while Callie did her eyebrow raise, insistent face best to encourage her in silence.

"Okay," I said. "Do I need one drink or two for this talk?" I was joking, of course, though I'd refrained from my usual pre-dinner gin and cranberry, wanting my wits about me, the matching mournful expressions—Callie's tinted with urgency—sparked me to jump in.

"My grandfather passed away," Thalia finally blurted, her thin, pale hands clasping together neatly on the counter. She'd been raised in the richest family in Wallace, old New England money, and spoke far more formally than most young women her age, always had, ever since she and Callie became friends as little girls. Polite to a fault and reserved, such a contrast to my rambunctious and talkative daughter, I was often reminded of the opposites attract stereotype they fit to a T.

"I'm so sorry, Thalia." I hugged her again,

wishing I could tuck her under my chin like I used to when she was younger. She'd long outstripped my 5'3", though the frail feel of her had never changed.

She clung to me a moment like she used to, reminding me she might be a grown woman now, but the child in her still lingered. "He's been sick for several months," she said, letting me go, head down, pushing her long, blonde hair behind her ear, full lips pressed together as her eyes moistened with unshed tears. "I hadn't seen him in a while, not since Mom and Dad." She stopped before the obvious, leaving that hurt lingering along with the fresh loss. Thalia hesitated, met Callie's eyes, the two linking in a shared moment I wasn't a part of. The muses, these girls, that fact the reason they'd become friends at first, the bond that I watched grow over the years never faltering. I was positive it was Calliope's support that kept Thalia together when Doncaster and Celia Vesterville were murdered three years ago, the gunman never caught. They'd raised her apart from the family, if you could call it that, their continual travels while Thalia was left to manage in their impressive house surrounded by nannies and servants a far cry from my idea of childrearing. Which naturally meant the shy and quiet child felt more like a daughter to me than just a friend of Calliope's. Their deaths when she was eighteen meant she needed my kid—and me, it turned out—more than ever.

"It's still a loss, Lia," I said. "Did you want to talk?" Bella had finished her dinner and hopped up on the counter, green eyes focused on the swaying young woman who hugged herself and shook her head, though when she noticed the cat staring she instantly reached out and lifted Belladonna into her arms, loud purring underscoring her words when she answered.

"No, it's all right, thank you." Again that look exchange with Calliope who finally exhaled an impatient little snort and spoke for her.

"The reading of the will is tomorrow," my daughter said. "Lia hasn't had much to do with the family for ages, but the executor guy—"

"Cousin Albert," Thalia said softly into the cat's fur.

"Yeah, him," Callie said, "insists she be there because there's some kind of thing in the will that says she has to be present in order to receive her inheritance." My daughter's opinion of the entire issue didn't need vocal articulation, the irritation and protective vibe practically pulsing from her spoke everything in a look and the tight line of her mouth. Not to mention I knew her well enough she didn't need to tell me she was unhappy and resistant.

"If Grandpa Reginald wanted me to be there, I should go." Thalia's hesitancy had me nodding.

"They're all jerks," my daughter blurted. "Everyone knows it."

"Not all of them," Thalia said in the quietest voice I almost missed it as I did my best not to sigh and chastise my daughter.

"Callie," I said. She scowled at me before backing down. "The Vesterville family deserves our condolences, not our judgments, right now."

She tossed her head, curls bouncing. "Whatever." The instance she spoke, she winced, my immediate irritation at that word reminding me so much of her father I had to clench my teeth to keep from responding in a way that wouldn't be helpful. Want to annoy me to no end? Tell me *whatever*. Just try it.

Calliope, for her part, relented with a regretful expression. "Sorry, Mom," she said. "I'm just, they're so mean, I don't want Lia…" She stuttered through a few thoughts then tossed her hands, glaring at her friend. "It's not like you need the money."

Thalia kissed Belladonna on the forehead before setting her gently back on the counter.

"I know," she said. "And I won't be alone. Uncle Gaines came home for it and he hasn't been around for ages. Not since…" Her turn to end halfway through a thought. She met my eyes then, blue ones uncertain, anxious. Too much weight on those narrow shoulders, the poor dear. "Not since Mom and Dad's funeral." The fact she said it out loud gave me hope. "I'll go," she said, "but I was hoping…"

"Mom," Callie interrupted, "she can't go alone. And I can't go with her. It's family only." Which meant what? "But you could."

"I'm not family either, sweetheart," I said.

Thalia smiled then, a brilliant and bright light that crossed her face and found her eyes and lit her up in a way I didn't see very often. Like someone flipped a switch and winter melted instantly in a lovely summer day through her.

"You will always be family," Thalia said. Okay, now I was going to cry. "But I know what you mean." She took one more glance at my biological daughter then rushed into the real reason they were here. "I checked and I'm allowed representation. I don't want a lawyer or anything." Thalia's sadness returned. "Callie suggested maybe you could come with me. As my counselor."

Oh, boy.

CHAPTER TWO

My initial instinct was to say no. Don't judge me or jump to conclusions that lead you to believe I didn't care or was intentionally cruel. Let me explain. From the moment they met, Thalia had always been the more vulnerable of the two girls. In fact, my daughter had gotten herself into trouble on the playground to that end, when a boy bullying Thalia found out what my daughter thought of such behavior, using her fist on his nose when words didn't suffice. And while I didn't condone violence, the contrast between the two had endured with Thalia looking to Calliope for strength, letting my daughter speak for both of them the majority of the time, struggling with her own self-confidence enough I worried about her and encouraged my own kid to back off at times so Thalia could find her voice.

Not that it always helped, though as they got older, I think Calliope understood better why it was important. But the precedent was set and regardless of what was good for Thalia, they had established their own little hierarchy only the two of them understood completely.

Which led me to the present and my thought process, not just as a mom, but a therapist (so often impossible to separate the two I stopped trying). This seemed to me an excellent opportunity for Thalia to do just that—establish boundaries inside the family she rejected out of old hurts and fears I knew just enough about to want her to find courage to deal with them once and for all. And while I understood completely her desire to have someone as backup in a difficult situation, how big of a disservice would I be doing her if I said yes?

On the other hand, what new pain would I be sending her into if I said no?

She must have seen the conflict on my face. Normally, my therapist expression remained calm and supportive, but this was Thalia, for goodness sakes. I was hardly subjective when it came to her. She was practically my kid as much as Calliope was, grew up in the house I'd shared with Trent all those years, the two girls the center of my life when he traveled for work more often than not. So, yes, it had to have been visible, this push/pull between wanting to protect her and wanting her to find her way to her own power.

"It's okay if you can't or don't want to, Seph." Her expression hadn't changed, the utter lack of disappointment hurting more than if she'd fought for me to join her. As though she expected a negative outcome which I knew had been embedded in her from the neglect of her parents, the past I'd done as much as I could over the years to heal while knowing there was only so much I could do regardless of my desire to help her. "It was just an idea. And like I said, Uncle Gaines has always been different from the others. He and Dad were close, as much as they could be with the two of them off traveling the world to avoid the family." Is that what her parents told her?

"The same Uncle Gaines who has a giant rep for spending way too much money, partying with Saudi princes and being kicked out of foreign countries for breaking the law?" Calliope wasn't just laying that out for Thalia, but for me, doing everything she could to trigger me. When had she become such a master manipulator?

Thalia stepped back a half pace, face set, mind made up. "I'll be fine." She smiled at Calliope, though I could see the trembling of her lower lip, the soft waver in her entire being as she nodded to both of us. "I'm going to head home. Thank you for the offer of dinner, but I'm not very hungry."

I almost went after her as she hurried out, guilt battling the therapist inside me who knew this was for the best. Even as my daughter glared at me with enough anger, she made up for the punishing prodding I was enduring internally for saying no when my entire being wanted to say yes.

Sometimes being a responsible adult who only wanted the best for the people in her life really sucked.

"You have no idea how horrible they are," Calliope said, now blinking her own tears, accusation in her voice, in the tension of her body, lashing out from fear for her friend while I nodded, staying quiet and letting her vent. "She cries just thinking about being around them, Mom. How can you let her go into that alone?"

I inhaled a long, slow breath, let it out at the same tempo. "Callie," I started.

"No, Mom." My daughter slapped one hand down on the counter, making Belladonna squeak and jump down out of her way, anger humming between us. "I know what you're going to say, that this is some life lesson, that she's twenty-one and a grown woman and all that stupid therapy bla bla bla." I did my best not to be offended because she was upset, let it go while she ranted on. "She needs you, Mom. Lia really needs you. I can't believe you right now." Before I could say a word, Calliope grabbed her jacket and spun, stomping to the door and slamming it behind her while I practiced my deep breathing a couple more times just to keep from swearing out loud.

In my head? Yeah, that was impossible.

It wasn't until I opened the cabinet door and realized I was out of gin I found myself scowling despite the calming method and might have let a bad word slip. Glanced at Belladonna who paused in her face cleaning to eye me like she disapproved.

"Sorry," I said. "Be right back." And headed for the door, keys and wallet in hand, sliding into my black leather jacket and then my SUV because tonight was going to require at least one drink while I figured out how best to support both of my girls.

Thing was, I had one hundred percent faith in Thalia. She might not have considered herself strong, but I knew better. After being raised like an afterthought and still turning out as a brilliant and caring young woman, not to mention the fortitude she showed when her parents were murdered, I had no doubt she'd be even stronger for facing down her family. But I couldn't help second-guessing myself, Momma Bear protectiveness roaring and then grumbling and then bellowing again in that short five-minute drive to the store demanding I get off my therapist high horse, forget the life lesson and stand between her and any kind of danger so she'd never have to deal with anything that made her feel vulnerable or unsafe ever.

I parked outside the market, mind in turmoil, tucking my keys into the pocket of my black dress pants, still in my work clothes though I knew the cropped motorcycle jacket I wore made me look like a middle-aged woman trying too hard and not caring even a little bit. Paused as I noticed two women standing half a block away outside the only expensive clothing boutique in Wallace, taking in the antagonism of their encounter physically if not audibly, their voices low enough I missed what they were saying, coming through loud and clear despite their attempt to keep the contents from the outside world. If the tall, skinny woman with the excessively dyed blonde hair and equally excessive makeup for a late Friday afternoon in a small town in Maine tried to hold back her sheer vitriol any longer, she'd probably have an aneurism. As for the exceedingly pregnant young woman half her age draped in enough fur and silk and diamonds for a 50s gala if a bit much for an early November afternoon, her baby was going to demand to be born that instant just to escape the vibrating distaste and borderline hate she veneered with just enough disdain to make it acceptable in public.

"We'll just see about that tomorrow, Shea" the older woman said, voice finally raised, veiled anger so thin it cut the air all the way to me.

"Yes, we really will, Eleanor," the younger woman said, chin jutting her aggressiveness, hands settling protectively over her bump.

Before either could say another word, the rumble of an engine cut them off, a tall, dark-haired man in a black Bentley pulling to the curb, cutting off two pedestrians and another car trying to park. He ignored the near accidents he'd caused, the beeping of the other vehicle, waving imperiously at the women. Eleanor tossed her hair, the spray she'd used to fuse the big waves giving her locks a stiff bounce instead of a flowing wave. "I can't wait to see you get what's coming to you tomorrow." She marched to the Bentley, climbing into the passenger's seat, slamming the door before the man peeled away, again so arrogantly oblivious to the world around him he narrowly missed an older woman with a walker and two cars navigating the parking spaces nearby.

Not to be outdone, the giant limo that pulled up took over the area while I stood there, chest tight, stomach churning, mind flat and angry, the driver exiting in his black suit and hat, guiding the pregnant Shea to the back of the car, helping her inside before driving away, the bulky vehicle taking up enough space for a jet liner.

Which they likely had in their arsenal, too. Because I'd just witnessed Eleanor Vesterville arguing with her mother-in-law—yes, I said that right, the very young and very pregnant widow of the now-deceased Reginald Vesterville and Thalia's grandfather—before Chairman Vesterville in his look at me Bentley made an appearance that decided everything.

My phone was in my hand before I knew I'd reached for it, speed dialing a number I knew by heart despite the fact it was already saved in my contacts.

I spoke before Thalia could say hello. "I'd

love to come," I said. "What time do I meet you tomorrow?"

Mamma Bear roared her approval.

CHAPTER THREE

I pulled up the long, winding drive to Vesterville House just before 1PM the next afternoon, after spending the evening assuring myself that I was mentally and emotionally prepared to not only support Thalia in whatever way she needed but had myself firmly under control. Because I kid you not if even one of her grossly arrogant and entitled family members said a single derogatory thing about her, I'd not be held responsible for the Kodiak rumbling inside me.

Come at me, bro.

The tall, perfectly manicured hedges lining the cobbled driveway remained green despite the near-empty trees above, only a few red and gold leaves still clinging to the towering oak trees that shielded the main house from the road on the other side of the massive stone wall and iron gate keeping the rest of us from the grounds. The drive widened suddenly to the open front lawn and sweeping entry to the estate's main house. Itself made of cold, gray rock and oppressively dominating height and width, I felt myself shrinking in the shadow of it though this was hardly the first time since I'd set foot here.

My SUV door hit a little hard when I closed it, the tension in my shoulders and jaw already building despite myself. How had I even considered letting Thalia deal with this on her own? If a building had a dour or ominous feel to it, Vesterville House did, as though a threat awaited within its walls for whoever braved the wide front steps, the looming columns, the tall windows like eyes watching, judging, assessing worth.

I had to get a grip already. It was just an old mansion. And this wasn't about me.

As I strode with a firm grasp on my intuition toward the double-doored entry, movement to the left distracted me from that sensation the house itself had seen into my soul and found me wanting. The driver from last evening leaned against the limousine parked at the other side of the curve, arms crossed over his chest, watching me. I waved, not out of politeness, but because it made me uncomfortable and nothing put a stop to that like taking action. He seemed startled and waved a little back. The smile that generated got me to the front door without scrunching myself under the pressure of the house's grim air.

A lean, dour-looking man with silver hair and a long, pointed nose opened the door to my ring, gong-like chime reaching me through the wooden doors preceding his arrival.

"Persephone Pringle," I said. "It's Lloyd, isn't it?" My terrible memory for names wasn't getting any better with age.

"Yes, ma'am, and how kind of you to remember." Whew, for once. He smiled faintly, gesturing for me to enter. "Welcome back to Vesterville House, Ms. Pringle." How he knew I wasn't a Mrs. anymore I wasn't sure. Maybe he called every woman Ms., but regardless, the mutual respect seemed to linger in a positive way that relieved some of my tension. I stepped inside as he went on. "Ms. Thalia will be down presently. Should I have one of the maids escort you to her room?"

"No need, Lloyd, thank you." I looked up as I entered, the towering foyer of Vesterville House the size of a normal person's home, two-story ceilings of dark wood panels offering none of the airy, spacious feel they could have if a lighter color, everything in the space either black marble (the floors) or dark stained hardwood (walls, giant staircase with massive railings that split like a T at the two levels it reached) and only adding to the gloomy, sorrowful feeling that was Thalia's hereditary home.

She hurried toward me, already at the bottom of the steps when she spoke, her flats making tapping noises on the polished floors, hands outstretched, looking fragile and almost translucent in her pale pink dress. While Thalia had always seemed vulnerable, her usual light shone through, the sunny heart of her the most attractive thing about her. The home she'd lived in with (and without) her parents, while large and palatial, didn't have the same old historical hurt absorbed deep into its bones. Here in Vesterville House, she looked drained of that illumination, her brilliance devoured by the hungry dimness welcoming her back to the fold and the place she'd started her life.

The fact her grandfather maintained a suite for her here said a lot about the possessiveness of this family. Or maybe it was the building itself, whispering insidious allure back to the belly of the beast, making a Vesterville's return inevitable?

I really had to stop imagining the estate house in such terms. Anthropomorphizing a building with human characteristics didn't help matters, and I was supposed to be here for Thalia, to keep her calm and comfortable, not working myself up for no reason.

Keep telling yourself that, Persephone. And don't let the creepy house eat your soul.

Thalia hugged me, smiling on the outside but trembling in her touch. I embraced her with all the confidence I could muster and smiled back when she let me go.

"Thank you for being here," she said, voice low.

"And who is this vision you've led astray, my darling niece?" I looked up in surprise, not realizing we weren't alone. To say he was handsome was to describe a fresh, ripe Maine strawberry as a piece of fruit. The man exuded charm and charisma, tied firmly to a cleft chin, chiseled jawline, blue eyes, deep brown hair swept from his broad forehead in a casual wave, navy blue suit jacket over a crisp white dress shirt and dark jeans showing off all the perfect angles of his wide-shouldered, narrow hipped body.

Never mind he was maybe thirty-five. Don't blame a girl for looking.

"Uncle Gaines." Thalia dimpled, so his

charms worked on her as well, though not the same way. He paused as he came to a halt next to us, bending to kiss her cheek with tender kindness, big hand on her shoulder, before turning that million-watt smile of perfect white teeth that reached those gorgeous cobalt eyes on me. "This is Persephone Pringle."

"Ah, finally," he said in his deep, velvety voice that could have made him millions in Hollywood. Did he really take my hand (did I offer it?) and kiss the back of it while holding my gaze in his until I was, dare I say, breathless? "I've never had the pleasure, though Thalia has talked endlessly of you and your charming daughter, Calliope. Doncaster and Celia's funeral simply seemed the worst time to make your acquaintance and I wasn't here long enough to pursue the point." He held my hand (was he going to give it back? Did I want him to?) as he smiled down at Thalia, his height at least a foot taller than mine, that sort of towering but protective presence in a large man that made me feel safe instead of intimidated. "Thank you for taking such good care of our Thalia all these years." When he returned his focus to me (knees, don't fail me), his expression softened to sorrow. "I am well aware," his voice lowered to include just the three of us though if there were others present,

I was positive they could pinch me and I wouldn't notice, "my dear brother and his wife were absent more than present even before their tragic loss." He squeezed my hand (yes, he was still touching me and if he didn't stop soon, I wasn't responsible for what happened). "I'm just as guilty. My own pursuits keep me away from home and my dear girl here." Gaines tapped the tip of Thalia's nose with one fingertip as though she was still little. Instead of responding negatively, she giggled. "It means the world to me knowing she has the two of you to lean on in these troubled times."

Was it wrong I almost protested when he finally let me go? So wrong. Dear heavens he was gorgeous and smelled so good I could barely catch my breath.

"Thalia is family," I said, on autopilot. Good thing my default wasn't an awkward weirdo. Um, most of the time. What was wrong with me? It wasn't like I hadn't been around a handsome younger man before.

Gaines leaned in, his scent, far from overpowering, overpowering. Phew, hot flashes anyone? "That makes us family," he said, voice dropping further, smile curving from charisma to sultry so fast my brain stopped functioning.

A door slammed, thank God. Jerked me out

of whatever spell the man cast over me, drew all of our attention toward the other side of the foyer, Eleanor and Chairman storming across the marble on their way toward the far side, followed by Shea and a short, roundish man I recognized as Albert Stewart, the family financial advisor and Thalia's cousin. The sight of the other Vestervilles was more than enough to break me out of whatever weird trance I'd been in, though just looking at Gaines had my insides turning to jelly all over again.

Who knew I'd be hormonally defenseless at my age? Then again, it wasn't like I was married anymore and fifty was the new thirty, right?

Snort. I was a therapist, and I needed my own head examined.

"It appears the family has decided it's safe for everyone to be in the same room together." Gaines winked at me, grinning at his niece who eye-rolled and tucked her arm through his when he offered. I declined taking the other when he extended his crooked elbow, hoping I strode next to them with what came across as confidence while my wobbly knees did their best to hold me up.

Apparently, I'd reverted to a teenager at some point and really needed to sort that out before I embarrassed myself.

Gaines paused at the doorway to the room

the others entered, releasing Thalia and gesturing for us to go in ahead of him. I hoped the sidelong glance I gave him on the way by didn't come across as flirty, but from the wicked smirk he gave me I failed miserably.

Oh well, a little harmless fun in a dark hour never hurt anyone, right?

CHAPTER FOUR

I followed Thalia, letting her choose where we sat, tucking in next to her on the leather sofa under a row of bookshelves reaching the fifteen-foot ceilings, rug under my feet quieting the high-heeled boots I'd worn, not bothering to shed my leather jacket as I sat back and crossed my legs, the rest of the family seated and sniping among themselves.

Funny that Chairman chose to sit alone in the large leather wingback in the center of the room facing the heavy, substantial carved desk under the tall windows framed with deep blue velvet curtains. Then again, I suppose it wasn't all that shocking he left his wife to find her own seat, arrogance etched in permanent lines across Chairman's face. Where his younger brother Gaines had that polished and stunning look of the Vesterville men of youth, Chairman's fifteen years seniority had shown the result of living in this particular family, a set of impressive jowls, protruding belly and faint line of dye along his thinning hairline only accentuating the truth he'd had some work done to minimize his aging process. I knew for a fact he was my age, had bumped into and briefly encountered him growing up here in Wallace, though our circles were very much different. I compared my ex-husband and his aging attractiveness and still-trim FBI issue figure to the tall and formerly handsome Chairman and had to wonder if having this much money and privilege was more a curse than a boon.

Helped me pull myself back together when I glanced behind him at Gaines seated in another wingback near the door, seeing his brother's fifteen years layered on him. Until he caught me looking and smiled.

Nope. Never going to happen.

"Are we going to do this or not?" Shea's whining turned my head, gaze finding her where she perched on a sofa across from Thalia and myself, the horseshoe setup of seating forcing Eleanor to either stand or sit on the other end of that same sofa. Which she did, looking like she'd have preferred a bed of snakes to lie down in, while glaring at Thalia for taking her preferred seat. You snooze, you lose, lady, could have sat long before we got there. Instead, they'd all been waiting, as if being the first to take a seat was a sign of weakness. The young widow's hands traced over the thin, black fabric of her dress, soothing the baby within in as familiar a maternal gesture as there ever was. I just hoped the kid had a chance to turn out like Thalia instead of the sour and petulant girl—yes, girl—who carried yet another Vesterville around.

"I'm sure Albert is getting to it," Gaines said of the financial cousin who stood behind the desk, preparing paperwork, a black urn with the silver Vesterville logo placed at the forefront. Reginald obviously wanted them to know he was still with them. "Shea, be a dear. Hand me that bowl of almonds."

She shot him a nasty look, the side table next to her set up with fruit, water glasses and various other snacks, the clear bowl half full of the nuts he requested. "Get your own."

"Your spoiled brat is showing again," Eleanor snapped.

Shea was an equal-opportunity sniper, looking down her nose at her daughter-in-law like she wasn't half her age. "And so is your b—"

"Enough!" Chairman's deep voice, a close match to his brother's but without the charm, shut them both down. "I'm sick of the two of you arguing."

Shea, to my surprise, went quiet, sullen, grabbing the bowl and extending it to Gaines a room away. Refusing to stand or make any other effort. I felt Thalia tense beside me, fought off the wash of respect as the handsome youngest Vesterville stood in a smooth motion and crossed to take the bowl from Shea's impatient hand.

"Thank you," he said, like she hadn't just slighted him.

"Sit down, Gaines," she snapped.

He spun, retreating to his own seat, pausing next to Chairman while examining the nuts inside the bowl.

"You heard Shea," his brother growled. "Go sit. Good dog."

Gaines didn't move, vicious smile replacing the charming one in an instant. I should have been grateful really, to witness the transformation, to feel my reaction toward him cool to a soft simmer, the truth of his own darkness flashing across his handsome face now as threatening and ominous as the house around us. "Dear brother," Gaines said, "you lost the right to tell me what to do a long time ago. Don't think just because I came home at Father's request you can start over. It doesn't work like that."

"We'll see," Chairman said. "When you find out he's cut you out of the will."

"Or maybe you're worried he cut you out," Gaines said, still with that horribly focused smirk on his face. He shook the bowl again, the moment broken as he looked down at the almonds, hand poised to choose one. "Wouldn't that be just like Father?"

Chairman's low growl silenced everyone. He reached up and grabbed the bowl from his brother, taking a fistful of the nuts and stuffing them into his face, chewing aggressively. "I said *sit.*"

That long moment they stared at one another? Lasted at least a decade, I swear. I didn't realize I'd been holding my breath until Thalia's hand squeezed mine, her rigid body reminding me I wasn't here for the spectacle.

Gaines finally barked a short laugh, shrugged and returned to his seat, that long stride carrying him quickly but smoothly until he settled once more, picture of elegance and poise, one hand cupping his cheek as he waited for the show to start.

"Ahem." Finally, something else to focus

on. I felt the entire room's tension ease in a wash of not quite relief but close enough while Albert cleared his throat and circled the desk, an envelope in his hands. He paused next to the urn and gestured toward it as he spoke. "It was Reginald's desire we all assemble here today, the full family Vesterville, for the reading of his last will and testament."

"Yes, yes, get on with it." Chairman ate another handful of almonds, still worked up, cheeks reddened, brow furrowed. "We know why we're here." He coughed a little around the chewing he was doing, and I did my best not to watch, because *ew*.

"By all means," Gaines said from the back of the room, that edge to his voice remaining. "Though, Cousin Albert, I'm surprised you're included in that since no Vesterville ever openly welcomed your side of the family into the fold." He spread both hands in front of him, beaming a mocking smile. "Welcome."

"Gaines, I swear to *God*," Eleanor spun on him, face fixed in place with enough filler and injections to prevent her from scowling fully, but the act not entirely lost, "if you don't shut up, I'll—"

"You'll what, dear sister?" It was obvious to me why Gaines had come as I watched this encounter unfold. How long ago had he left?

Harboring enough animosity and anger toward the others and finally presented the opportunity to unleash it in his own taunting way? This family really was a disaster waiting to happen. "Please, do tell. Considering dear old Dad managed to begat another Vesterville on young Shea there before he kicked off while you and Chairman fell short in that department, you're hardly in a position to silence anyone." He glanced slyly at Thalia. "Unlike Doncaster and Celia, I might add."

Wow, youch. Thalia twitched next to me, pale but for two pink points at the tips of her cheekbones, eyes downcast, lips a thin line despite their usual fullness. All respect I had for Gaines vanished, as did my attraction. He was no different from the rest of them, was he? For all his charm and charisma, he just used Thalia against his sister-in-law at the dear girl's expense. For the last time.

I hoped he caught the flat look I shot him because he'd be getting that and a mouthful later, you better believe it.

As for Eleanor, she spluttered, looked to Chairman who was too busy angrily munching on almonds, spite-eating his brother's selection, to offer assistance. She finally fell still, leaning back with her arms crossed and her face in a fixed glare of fury.

Albert's visible discomfort and lack of commanding presence weren't helping any. I had to fight off the urge to tell him to hurry the heck up already when he finally did go on in a blurting attempt to regain control of the moment, faint sheen of sweat showing on his upper lip and the balding top of his head through his silvered hair drawing attention to his lack of authority despite the dark gray suit and tie and the position he held at the front of the room.

"Shall we begin?" He cracked the seal, real wax, how archaic, the Vesterville crest in black on the back of the envelope making a snapping sound when he broke it. Paper rustled, a single sheet, how odd. Even Albert seemed surprised by the lonely stationary piece he held in his hands, reading aloud in a trembling voice. "To my family, for what that word is worth, herein is the sum and total of your inheritance, designed personally and with great care for each of you. You are each now the proud owners of a key of my choosing, a key that will open a box of my design. Only when said key and box are combined will your inheritance be uncovered. Reginald."

CHAPTER FIVE

The following silence? Deafening. I'd heard that term used before, thought it was a fallacy, someone's imagination tapping into a flair for the dramatic. But until that moment, I had no idea sudden quiet could feel like the whole world emptied out and nothing remained behind but shock and nothingness.

Of course, it lasted about as long as it took the Vestervilles to draw breath (all but Thalia) and begin their loud protesting. Their shouting was almost worse, mingling voices blurring together as their words, while varying in content, all struck the exact same chord over and over. There was enough anger in that room to crush an elephant under the pressure of it. Despite my detachment from the family's predicament—I wasn't about to inherit anything, after all—I couldn't fully defend against the onslaught of all that vitriol, like a wave of barely buried garbage heaving to the surface to smother all light and air.

No wonder the young woman beside me sagged a little, meeting my eyes when I turned to focus on her partially for my benefit, the distress she'd been fighting since we sat down faded to surprise and a hint of a grin.

Hang on a second. She was *enjoying* this?

Until Chairman stood, the bowl of almonds hitting the floor with a thud as he discarded it, nuts scattering under the sofa in a pattering dance beside him as his booming voice dominated. "This is preposterous! I won't be party to a ridiculous attempt to circumvent the law. Where is the real will?"

Albert's spluttering turned to what looked like anxious fear to me when Chairman stepped forward and grabbed the page from him, scanning it while Albert turned rather quickly and lifted a small box from the table. Held it out in front of him rather like a shield in defense, to show he wasn't responsible for what came next, perhaps. Long, black lacquered, laced with silver and the Vesterville crest, he cradled it in his hands less like a precious memento and more like proof of life.

"That's all there is, Chairman," he said in

the sniveling tone I associated with those who knew they had no ground to stand on in the face of their betters and learned a long time ago exactly how much they were worth. It turned my stomach, frankly, but didn't stop Albert from extending the thing he held as an offering to the man he must have seen as worthy. "And this box."

But, before the eldest Vesterville son could grab it from Albert and take over the proceedings (more than likely a common occurrence for Chairman, the type of person whose bullying attitude always meant he got his way), Gaines somehow magically crossed the room (okay, he was probably on the move all along, but Chairman's actions kept my attention until he reached them) and put himself firmly between his older brother and cousin.

That had to be a shock for the so-called head of the family because Chairman didn't protest when his youngest and only living brother blocked his way. I felt my own estimation of Gaines rise further, the fact he was willing, among all of them, to stand up to the domineering and supposed heir to the family fortune not exactly making him a hero but at least elevating him well past the remainder of the Vestervilles.

Thalia, from the grin that hadn't yet left her face, clearly approved.

"I believe," Gaines said in a low and threatening voice, so far from the smooth allure of his normal tone I felt my eyes narrow, mind turning, "there are keys to be passed out. Boxes to be found. And answers, I warrant, to be uncovered, all courtesy of Father. Who always had a rather odd sense of humor, wouldn't you agree, dear brother?" He stood there, toe-to-toe with Chairman, the same height but leaner, stronger, younger than the elder. And, though Chairman's blustering and volume made him the perfect bully, there was something dangerous about Gaines that had me wishing his brother would just back off.

Which he did, finally, to my breath of relief. Not that I figured Gaines would hurt Chairman, but if someone could kill with a stare, the older brother should have been dead and gone.

Chairman sat heavily in the wingback, Gaines seating himself on the edge of the desk, pleasant smile replacing his previous expression so easily and with such practice I blinked in surprise, gesturing for Albert to carry on with his presence preventing further interruption.

The fact no one protested had me

wondering if the rest of the Vestervilles saw what I just did and were reassessing the man they likely underestimated as much as I had. Thalia's explanation of Gaines and his absence from the family didn't jive at all with the man I was observing now. While perhaps someone who spent his adult years traveling the world, wasting his trust fund on women and parties and adventure-seeking might develop a backbone at some point, there was clearly more to him than any of them had led themselves to believe.

Well, good for him. Maybe that meant this would all work out better than I'd hoped, and Thalia would at least have one ally in the family. Or, at the very least, not an enemy. Which, in this particular case amounted to the same thing as far as I was concerned.

Trust him? Not on your life. But allow him to take charge and shield Thalia from the others? In a heartbeat.

Though Chairman's actions left him visibly shaken, Albert proceeded when Gaines nodded for him to do so, still looking for the boss of him, I suppose. Regardless the cousin's motives, he settled somewhat before opening the box with a little flair of dramatic handwork before pulling out a beautifully made silver key with a black tag hanging from it. Everyone stared while he examined the silver-rimmed label that matched the implement he held. "Number one," he said with enough relief he still understood who his real master was, gaze lifting to the eldest son who glowered, fidgeting in his seat. "For Chairman."

He took it with a grunt, though he didn't rise, forcing Albert to deliver it. Honestly, the man was insufferable. And if he didn't get that temper of his under control, face still red, jaw jumping as he cleared his throat but didn't comment, he was going to give himself a stroke.

Not the worst outcome, maybe.

Persephone Pringle. Shame on you.

Next came a bronze key with a brown tag, also lined in the same metal. "Number two is for Eleanor." Albert licked his lips, meeting her eyes with his own softening, while I had a funny feeling in the pit of my stomach there was a secret there my intuition prodded me to uncover. I shushed it, because the only person of import in the room was sitting next to me. The rest of them could keep their mysteries.

Eleanor rose to accept it, unlike her still restless husband who seemed to wrestle with his fury, ignoring the rest of us as his fist clenched around the key in his hand, gaze on it and not the moment unfolding beside him. Her lips twisted in disgust when Albert offered up the item, though she palmed the four-inch key and pressed it protectively to her chest as she retreated back to the sofa. Her attempt at blasé crashed and burned, that acquisitive pinch to her lips and greed in her gaze as she quickly and furtively studied her key a dead giveaway.

Was money all that really mattered to these people? Getting what they deserved?

"Number three," Albert said of the copper key with the green tag. "For Shea."

She was close enough she didn't have to rise At least she was honest about her emotions, making no effort to hide her grabbiness, unlike Chairman and Eleanor, studying it with exasperation before tossing her hands and sighing heavily.

"Number four," he said, checking the blue tag on the gold key, "is for Gaines."

The handsome younger brother accepted his with a simple head nod, not looking, just sliding it into his inside pocket.

"Number five," Albert said, thick, dark brows rising in surprise at the name on the yellow tag dangling from what looked like a key made from aluminum, "is mine."

"Imagine that," Gaines murmured before falling silent again.

"And the last one," Albert said, lifting out a

dark gray key that looked like it might be steel, a deep purple tag attached, "is for Thalia."

I'd forgotten she was holding my hand, felt her squeeze as she rose, crossed to Albert, took the key then returned right to me, sitting again in prim perfection with the offering settled in her lap. Someone had gone to a lot of effort, the lovely key a thing of beauty, the deep purple of the tag outlined and hanging from a chain of the same metal. If there was a significance to the color and material chosen, and I had no doubt there was, I couldn't help but think of swords and royalty when I looked at hers.

"That's it." Albert seemed hesitant as he showed us the empty box, his own key already tucked away in his suit's inner pocket like Gaines had done.

"Not quite," the younger Vesterville brother said in that jovial good humor that hid all the hate and condemnation in the world behind those blue eyes and that delightful smile. "We have some boxes to find. Who's up for a treasure hunt?"

Chairman spluttered, face redder than ever, clearly furious about the whole thing. Though, when he half stood, hand clutching at the arm of the wingback, other extended toward Gaines as he gasped and choked, I had a panicked moment. Wait, was he angry or was there something—

He answered my question before it was done, crashing to the floor with a gurgling sound, clutching his throat convulsively before his entire body shuddered, lifting off the ground in a heaving protest.

I didn't even know I'd moved, the sound of Eleanor screaming, scent of Gaines next to me as I pressed my fingers into Chairman's throat and felt for a pulse while knowing it was too late and there was nothing I could do.

No light in those eyes. Dead giveaway. Wince, sorry, terrible wording. But true, nonetheless.

Chairman Vesterville wouldn't inherit a thing. Except maybe a fancy urn to match his father's.

CHAPTER SIX

Sheriff Cherise King listened carefully as I told her everything I'd seen, my attention drawn to the arrival of our local mortician, Owen Graves, who waved on his way by, our one-young-man forensics department and coroner clothed in a white coverall, dark curls hidden under the hood, blue plastic booties over his shoes matching the gloves on his hands. I stared at the silver case he carried, jumped a little at the sound of the EMTs bringing in the gurney, the echoing of the unfolding so loud I caught my breath and actually clutched at my chest like some B-movie starlet who was next to die in the haunted house.

Cherise's lovely alto was as gentle as ever, dark eyes catching mine, thick lashes rimming

her kind and caring gaze always making me
jealous. Only she could make the khaki sheriff's
uniform shirt look good, dark skin that deeply
glowing brown that would never age, thick,
black hair close-cropped so tight the wave of
the curls barely showed, giving her the
Amazonian warrior goddess look filled out by
her impressive height and build. The former
Chicago police detective turned Wallace town
sheriff might have been a hardened homicide
investigator where she came from, but this
wasn't my first body, either, unfortunately, nor
my first murder case.

If in fact, it *was* murder. I caught myself
glancing at the open doorway where I'd
previously sat with Thalia, knowing she was
safe and sound, Callie's arrival at my call just
before Cherise and the ambulance pulled up
guaranteeing the youngest Vesterville would
have the comfort she needed while I spoke to
the sheriff.

Tried to speak. Stumbled a few times when
distracted. Had to finally inhale slowly while
Cherise waited in that bottomless patience of
hers, exhaling at last while I reached out and
squeezed her wrist to ground myself to reality.

"He may have choked," I said. Or had that
stroke I'd horrifically suggested might be a
good thing and could only now dwell on with

a sick feeling in my stomach. "He'd been eating almonds." But he'd discarded the bowl. Unless he had one still in his mouth, he should have been fine. "He was pretty worked up at the end. Possible heart attack or even a stroke." Yup, there was that accusatory word spoken out loud. I shook my head. "I don't know. It happened so fast. By the time I got to him, his heart had stopped." I let her go, blinking, knowing I shouldn't be feeling guilty in the moment but not able to halt the wash of it that gripped me while I fought for air and stability as Cherise just stood and held space and supported me with her presence. "I was going to start CPR, but Eleanor was so upset, she pushed me aside. I didn't get to try." Something I'd carry with me the rest of my life. Along with the worry I'd given in too easily, perhaps. As much as I wanted to believe I would have given my best to save him, a part of me would always fear I'd backed down because of who he was.

Silly to worry about such things but being present during death when there was even a chance and doing nothing didn't sit well with me.

Cherise returned the touch, though mine had been rather desperate, needing her to anchor me so I wouldn't lose it. Hers offered support and love and the friendship and mutual adoration we had for each other, calming me more than words would have.

She didn't get to speak, Owen swishing his way toward us, sliding to a halt on the shining floors in those ridiculous booties, his earnest face surrounded by the white elastic holding the hood over his clear plastic goggles, perched on his wide, freckled nose.

"Don't shoot the messenger," he said, "but looks like poisoning, boss."

Cherise's short nod answered. "You're sure?" I knew she wasn't questioning his abilities. The twenty-three-year-old had not only graduated from high school three years early, he'd aced his forensics program in two while studying medicine at the same time. Two years ahead of Calliope and Thalia, he'd always been a little awkward, and more than brilliant. While he may have been young, we were lucky to have him.

"Looks like cyanide," he said.

"He was eating almonds," I blurted. "The smell wouldn't tell you anything." That was right, wasn't it? Didn't cyanide resemble that scent?

He nodded, no more offended by my interruption than Cherise's question, pushing the goggles up his nose with one gloved finger, holding up a plastic bag with the other. He'd collected the nuts that remained, it seemed, innocuous things clustered into the corner of the baggie.

"Field test proved it," he said. Shrugged. "I'll take the body in for an autopsy, do a full panel, but I doubt it'll turn up anything different."

I caught my breath. "Gaines was going to eat those," I said. Turned to find him talking with a deputy. "Shea handed them to him."

Cherise noted that down while Owen gestured for the remaining Vesterville brother to join us. The tragedy of that wasn't lost on me, Gaines's now grim expression and visible distress making me question what I'd seen earlier. Was he really upset? He nodded to Cherise politely, then to me without a hint of flirting, looking down at the bag in Owen's hand with a small frown.

"Sheriff King," he said, "we haven't met. Gaines Vesterville."

She shook his hand, and the way her gaze lingered I knew his matching height and broad shoulders, not to mention that handsome face and incredible voice (did I mention how good he smelled?) had her noticing. Considering her equally tall and stunning husband, Dorian, was nothing to sneeze at, I felt better knowing I wasn't the only woman who felt the weight of Gaines Vesterville's charms.

"Mr. Vesterville," she said.

"Gaines, please." He flashed that smile and I almost grinned at the softening of Cherise's own. I'd be teasing her later, you bet I would, over a gin. While we giggled like girls about a cute boy.

Silly, but it would happen. And gave me a bit of relief in the thinking of it while she went on.

"Gaines. May I ask, did you eat any of these?" She pointed with her poised pen at the baggie Owen lifted one more time to show him.

Gaines shook his head slowly, that frown back but gloriously delicious in its intensity. I needed to focus. And not on him.

"Chairman helped himself before I could," he said, concerned now, meeting Cherise's eyes with his full of worry. "Why?"

"Mr.—Gaines. Have there been any threats against the family lately that you know of?" I looked back and forth between them, realizing why she was asking before turning in a short hit of panic to where Calliope sat on the staircase with her arm around Thalia, best friends leaning into one another while my brain went worst-case scenario.

There was an excellent chance Chairman wasn't the target and now I worried the whole family (okay, my two girls my only focus) was in danger.

Cherise didn't get to say so much out loud, Shea's grating voice echoing as she spoke loudly enough to silence everyone and draw attention.

"Is this almost over?" She glared at Cherise. "We were in the middle of something, you know."

Eleanor looked like she was going to lose it, tears streaming down her face, though I knew it was uncharitable to wonder if they were real tears or if she'd secreted some saline somewhere. Pers*ephone*. Bad therapist. But she didn't comment first, not quite fast enough on the uptake, perhaps overwhelmed with emotion or just not prepared.

Unlike her clever and charismatic brother-in-law who always seemed ready for anything. "Ah, yes," Gaines said. "Chairman's death getting in the way of your inheritance, Shea, my dear?"

She scowled at him, so close to a pout it hurt. "Well, he's dead and we're not and those boxes aren't going to find themselves." Even Shea seemed suddenly embarrassed, at least a little, going quieter as she spoke. "He'd have done the same if it was one of us."

"Touché," Gaines said. "And utterly accurate." He shrugged, turned back to Cherise. "The Vesterville family melodrama endures," he said. "Though step-mummy dearest is correct." Shea's face contorted at his cynical shot in her direction. "We are in fact, in the midst of uncovering what Father decided to give each of us. Or not."

"There's a possibility your brother's death was aimed at all of you," Cherise said, keeping her voice down, meant for Gaines. Did she see him as the responsible one? She had no idea. For his part, his guarded humor I was positive hid a lifetime of resentment and simmering bitterness that would take me years to unravel, faded into serious understanding, the first truly authentic expression I think I'd seen him wear.

"I see." He glanced away once, and only once, and in that moment redeemed himself in my eyes, his anxious expression focused on Thalia. Whatever his history in the family, whatever hurts he buried deep under that handsome exterior, knowing Gaines put her first? Made him the best of the Vestervilles.

Considering the lineup left over, however, it wasn't much of a contest.

"Once I've talked with everyone," Cherise raised her voice, heavy authority in her tone, "we will see about continuing your treasure hunt." Gaines's grimace was less amused and more annoyed, though not at her, I was sure.

I joined the girls in a rush, doing my best not to look scared, forcing calm I didn't feel as I sat next to them, hugging them both, Thalia between Calliope and myself, a little Vesterville sandwich center. She had started shaking when I'd returned to her after Eleanor drove me from the body and clearly hadn't stopped, Calliope's worried look and the approach of Gaines driving me back to my feet.

"I'll get you some tea." I would never admit to either of them I simply couldn't sit still, that the ridiculous idea tea might make her feel better was the only option that came to me, hurrying past Gaines who paused but didn't pursue and went in search of Lloyd and the kitchen.

CHAPTER SEVEN

So, while I might have had good intentions, my follow-through kind of sucked. Instead of locating Lloyd and tea, I promptly got lost in the maze-like warren of corridors that was the servant's area, startled to find it so different from what I knew of the main house. Only to stumble into the young driver as I came around a corner. He looked up from sorting through a cupboard, his expression showing his surprise at my sudden arrival. He closed the door firmly as I approached, enough guarded caution to his stance I couldn't help but wonder what he'd been up to and if I should tell Lloyd to count the silver.

Uncharitable of me, yes, but considering the day I was having? Surely, I got a pass.

To make up for my internal rebuke, I

overdid it to compensate because what was a little awkwardness between strangers in a creepy back hallway in a mansion of murder?

"Hi," I said, sticking out a hand in greeting. "Persephone Pringle."

It was my first really good look, the handsome if sullen young man's brown hair neatly trimmed, though I wondered if the scruff of day-old beard was up to Vesterville code, those light brown eyes watchful and guarded. He hesitated before shaking mine in return, rather weakly and without enthusiasm before dropping his hand. "Fielder Grant," he said, with a reluctance I found odd. What, did he find chatting with an older woman a useless effort? I had to remind myself through my jag of self-consciousness he *did* work for the Vestervilles. Maybe he thought that elevated him above needing to be polite to someone like me.

"Can you help me?" I chose to go for vulnerable, hoping his inner hero—what there was of it—would take pity on me despite his original attitude. I followed my question with a soft, sad laugh. "I'm looking for the kitchen." Tossed my hands in defeat and waited.

"This way, ma'am." So, he had a good guy in him, did he? Fielder reacted instantly, even smiling, as he gestured for me to turn around, leading me back the way I'd come.

"How long does it take to figure this place out?" My attempt at conversation had him frowning again.

"Not long," he said. Well, that was informative.

"Have you been with the family for a while?" Now I was curious, and could you blame me? He seemed rather young—maybe early twenties—to be trusted as a driver for the family.

Fielder shrugged. "Long enough," he said. Glanced at me, offered a vicious little grin. "One big happy family, huh?" Just as he pushed open a door to the kitchen where Lloyd, who obviously caught the cynical line, wore a frown of disapproval on his face.

"Mr. Grant," he said as though this weren't the first time he'd had to bring something of note to Fielder's attention. "We do not talk about the Vestervilles in such a manner if we wish to remain employed by them." The young driver, rather than appearing chastised, just turned and left, Lloyd sighing sadly. "No respect from young help these days," he said.

No comment. My request, instead, for tea, was met with immediate assurances, though when Lloyd turned away to tell the cook, I had a moment of compassion, touching his arm.

He spun back to me, face creased and weary and I realized despite the fact Chairman wasn't much of a human being, he and this family were Lloyd's life for many years.

"I'm so sorry," I said. "Never mind. I should have realized how hard this must be for you. For all the staff."

His face softened, lines from age and now the death of his employer so recently receding as much as the white hair on his head. "This family's tragedies know no end, Ms. Pringle," he said. "To lose Mr. Chairman so soon after Mr. Reginald…" he tsked softly. "While many judge them for their manner, this family and this house," he gestured to include the whole building, not just the warm kitchen we stood in, "has become my home as much as theirs." He nodded once, composure returning. "Ms. Thalia shall have her tea in short order. And my service, as always."

The old dear was going to make me cry. I left him when he urged me to return to the girls, finding it easier to make my way back than arrive, emerging from the hallway leading to the back of the house into the foyer with a little sigh of relief. Just as Shea, her patience clearly used up, stormed past Cherise and up the stairs.

"I'm going to my room to lie down," she

told no one in particular. "All this fuss is bad for the baby." She stomped as she went, surely just as harmful to the unborn child, but I wasn't saying so. I watched her climb in a huff, slowing a little as she ran out of steam, but made it without mishap to the second floor, heading off to the right and disappearing where the corridor led to the residential wing.

No one seemed to care, two deputies and Cherise wrapping up, it seemed, since before I could reach the girls still sitting on the bottom stair, the sheriff parted ways with Eleanor Vesterville and came to me, head down, while her two young officers tipped their hats and left through the front door.

"Here's the thing," my friend said in a low, tense voice, smiling slightly, likely as a ruse. I was in, of course, I was. "I've had issues with the Vestervilles in the past." Do tell, Cherise. "They have a tendency to lawyer up." Case in point, I assumed. "Eleanor is the family legal representative, and she tends to lean toward the overly cautious no matter what the situation." I hadn't realized she was a lawyer, interesting. And had no doubt my friend was understating what was likely a more serious frustration with the Vestervilles and their entitlement. What infractions had Cherise had to swallow so far? Had to rankle. "Which means, as much as it hurts, I have to tread lightly here." Wait, had they threatened her job in the past? We'd just see about that. "I need a favor, and I hate to ask, but you're all I've got."

"Anything," I said, suddenly so annoyed with the whole situation even my worry for Thalia was burned to ash because no wonder someone wanted to kill them all.

"You're staying, I take it? For the treasure hunt?" Gaines's reference had become the *nom de jour*. I nodded. "Just keep your eyes and ears open." She huffed a little breath. "Do not put yourself in danger. Do not do anything Trent will be angry with me for." My ex-husband might have been a mutual friend of, but he didn't get a say though I held off reminding her of that. "Do not put my investigation in any kind of jeopardy." She paused, shook her head. "This is a terrible idea."

I reached out, another wrist squeeze, reassuring this time. "Trust me," I said. "I have no desire to put myself into any situation remotely resembling the ones I've already endured." Nope, two killers under my belt were plenty, thanks. "If I hear anything, or see anything, I'll text you right away and you can deal with it. Okay?"

The hesitation in her black eyes faded. "Promise me."

I held up a pinky that made her snort, but she did a quick link up anyway. "What, are we six?"

"Um, you do know pinky swear is forever," I said, feigning offense.

"You're such a weirdo," she said. Laughed. Sighed like it hurt. "Don't make me regret asking." She brushed off my protest. "I'm going to do some digging into the family, the staff. Check for a trail on the cyanide. If I can find who acquired it and connect them to the family, it should tell us who the killer is."

"Do you think one of the family was involved?" That would be… very Vestervillian of them. Like, the ultimate in Vesterville behavior.

Cherise didn't seem to disagree. "There's no proof of that," she said. "More likely it's someone on staff or someone with a grudge. They have enough enemies, I'm sure." Sounded like she knew of a few reasons already. "But if you can watch for unusual behavior while I do my part, we might catch the killer."

"Unusual behavior." I let her see my eyebrow raise, hear the sarcasm while she grinned and shook her head. "Okie doke, Cherise. Like this whole freaking thing isn't unusual or anything."

"Keep a close eye on the girls," Cherise said. "I know, I don't need to tell you that. But if someone is targeting Vestervilles…"

She had to bring that worry up again, my Momma Bear emerging from hibernation to grunt her assurances no one would hurt my girls. Over my dead—

Persephone. You know better.

I watched Cherise leave, Owen and the EMTs leaving with the body, startled when Lloyd suddenly appeared at my side with a tray and whispered, "Ms. Thalia's tea, ma'am."

I spun on him, a sudden inspiration taking me over as I helped myself to the tray with a smile for him. "Can you bring another?" He nodded immediately while I went on. "And can you tell me, where is Shea's room?" After all, I couldn't keep my eyes open if she was out of sight, could I?

Time for a little visit with the expectant widow.

CHAPTER EIGHT

At least this time I didn't get lost, Lloyd's instructions clear enough, the upper floors of Vesterville House along the same palatial, grand lines as the first without the rabbit-like trail of corridors and rooms the staff made use of. The only trouble here was the quiet dimness, accentuated by the lack of anyone, simply one long, vast hallway that felt more like a museum than a home. I avoided looking up at the endless portraits taller than I was looming with their disdainful disapproval staring at one another across the again dark-wood paneled walls, the thick run of deep blue carpet a runway down the matching hardwood floors. I wondered if anyone stopped to use the antique chairs placed here and there along the way, if the window seat I encountered as I was guided to the left and into the depths of the wing was ever used to sit on quiet and rainy afternoons, staring out into the garden below. Hard not to feel like I'd been dropped into some kind of period movie where women sighed in dark corners tucked tightly into Victorian corsets and heavy dresses, reading poetry and longing for love unrequited. Or, worse if I let myself go there, the dreary and rather anxious expectation of one of those said Victorian women appearing and disappearing through doorways still firmly closed.

I'd never seen a ghost but if one showed up, Cherise and Thalia were both on their own.

I didn't get to reach Shea, barely breathing in the stillness, feeling far more intruder than guest. Fortunately for me, she wasn't in her room, the rustle of someone moving through a partially open door and the hissing sound of a voice stopping me in my tracks, the tea service rattling faintly on the silver tray as I did.

"And I'm telling *you*," she snarled with heat, cheeks pink from it, tossing aside cushions on what looked like a sofa in a sitting room on the other side of the door, "this is the only way to the money. Like it or not, we need to find those boxes." She went silent a moment, standing upright and pressing one hand to the small of her back with a soft groan though her anger hadn't diminished. "Just shut up and keep looking. Let me know the moment you find anything." She thumbed the hang-up button with some aggression before looking up.

To find me watching.

I acted before she could react, I held out the service, smiling faintly, rather enjoying the faint panic that crossed her face. "I thought you might like some tea."

Shea's initial reaction slammed into a wall of arrogance she'd clearly learned to cultivate, sweeping toward me, gesturing at the tray. "Take that away and leave."

Um, not your serving girl, darling pet. "You're welcome," I said.

Her shock at my retort hit my funny bone in a sad and pitying way that wasn't beyond me, therapist or not. Hey, I was human, too. And frankly, her attitude left so much to be desired it could take a flying leap when she did.

"I told you to leave," she snapped.

"Maybe if I worked for you," I said at my mildest, letting her see my amusement, "I'd think about doing as you asked. But I don't, Shea. I don't work for anyone but myself." Yeah, she loved that, let me tell you. From the sudden reddening of her face, scrunched nose and the line forming between her brows—so young for such a deep wrinkle, dear—she was about to throw an epic tantrum I just didn't have time for. "Maybe you and whoever it was you were talking to would like to reconsider treating me like your servant and instead start telling me what your real game is."

Instead of answering, that same rush of anxious worry showing for a moment when she realized I couldn't be bullied, Shea instead brushed past me, hitting the edge of the tray on purpose, forcing me to focus on keeping it upright in a rattling and sloshing near-disaster instead of dumping the contents on the floor as she fled.

Childish act, but not exactly unexpected. And now I had a clear suspect, if not for Chairman's murder, someone who wasn't necessarily putting the family first.

Thalia did say her step-grandmother was a gold digger. But the fact she had a partner in her activities that raised my suspicions to the type of heights that made one nervous and gave a hit of vertigo? That was something of note, sure was.

I headed back downstairs, seeing Shea moving at a clip ahead of me, watching her descend fast enough I worried about the baby. By the time I reached the foyer, she had cornered Eleanor near the study door and was talking fast and gesturing in my direction.

Eleanor's barely-there frown turned toward me, the unlikely duo likely aligning against me, though if Chairman's widow knew what Shea was really up to, I doubted she'd back the young woman. None of my business, except Cherise *made* it my business, didn't she?

Thalia and Callie had disappeared from the bottom of the stairs. I set the tray aside on a side table, not sure what else to do with it, and headed for Eleanor directly, Shea crossing her arms over her chest and glaring at me. While the younger woman didn't seem all the broken up over her stepson's passing, neither—and more importantly in my opinion—did his wife. In fact, grief had turned instead to calculated cunning and I knew as I came to a halt in front of them exactly what Eleanor was about to say.

"You're not family." She tossed that vigorously sprayed blonde do, the firmly held waves bouncing in one piece as she did, her own arms crossing as Shea's were, the enemies—make no mistake, they were far from friends—finding a united front to stand against before turning on one another again. "You may leave."

"No, Aunt Eleanor." I had expected to defend myself, not noticing Thalia and Callie had joined us. Wherever they'd been lurking, the youngest Vesterville wasted no time speaking up. I had to admit, I was delighted with her decision to stand up and be counted, noting the flash of anger in Eleanor's expression and wondered if this was the first show of backbone she'd seen from her niece. "Seph is here on my behalf. I invited her. And while she's not a Vesterville, she's *my* family." Thalia's tall, thin body stood firm, voice unshaken, chin up and eyes flat. "She goes when *I* say."

Eleanor spluttered, Shea glaring. "This is ridiculous," her lawyer aunt finally managed. "We have more important things to deal with than your need for therapy." Shea snorted at that, vicious gleam in her dark eyes, delicate face twisting with it.

I caught his scent before I heard him speak, Gaines's voice soft behind me, though firm enough as he interrupted.

"Then perhaps we should get back to it," he said, not a suggestion, hard-edged and commanding, far more than his older brother showed in the short time I'd been here. "You can go back to your infighting and sniping once the boxes are found." He took my hand, turned me gently around and nodded to me. "Seph, I know Thalia appreciates your presence and that of your lovely daughter and as long as I'm a Vesterville with a stake in all this, you are welcome here." So there. "If you would be so kind to assist in the search, I know this will move much more quickly with your help."

And that was that. I didn't miss the speculative and rather nervous recalculation in Eleanor's eyes, the way Shea looked back and forth between her and Gaines like she expected more and was sorely disappointed. The pregnant girl huffed and pushed between Gaines and me, muttering as she went some rather off-color words I wasn't sure were suitable for the baby to hear, unborn or not.

I half-expected (okay, wanted, get over it) Gaines to linger. Instead, he released me and turned, heading toward another doorway and entering, clearly on the hunt himself. Eleanor's gaze followed him until he disappeared, giving me one last glare and strode off with her heels clicking on the marble floor. That left me alone with Thalia and Calliope while the two held hands and stared at me in expectation.

"Thalia," I said. "How much do you know about Shea's past?"

She thought about it a moment before shaking her head, blonde hair shimmering over her shoulders before she pushed it back with her free hand. "Very little," she said. "I'm actually hoping she won't inherit anything, that Grandpa Reginald saw through her." Her eyes widened, mouth open in a small O of guilt. "I don't mean to be cruel. It's just, I know she was taking advantage of him. Everyone knew." She sighed deeply, sagging while Calliope slipped one arm around her waist, worried expression turned up toward her best friend. "I have all I need thanks to Mom and Dad. I don't want more money. All I want is to know who killed them, that's all." The unresolved murders weighed on her, I knew that. They'd died in California, however, so Cherise was unable to do much to assist and the LAPD hit a wall that meant the case had gone cold almost immediately after it happened. "But someone like Shea... she doesn't deserve to be rewarded for trying to take advantage of my grandfather."

I agreed, except. "I suppose that's not up to you," I said.

"Exactly." Calliope squeezed her then let her go, smile rounding her full cheeks further, a hint of excitement in my daughter easing the tension and the mood. "So, what do you say? Let's go on a treasure hunt."

Thalia seemed unable to muster enthusiasm but nodded. "Thank you both for being here for me," she said. "It means so much to me." I leaned in and hugged her, Calliope squeezing both of us and when we stood back from one another, Thalia seemed much more relaxed, even determined as she grinned grimly at Calliope. "Let's get this over with."

"Treasure hunt," my daughter said, rubbing her hands together, bouncing on her toes. "My favorite."

"Moving on with my life," Thalia said, touching Calliope's cheek with soft fingertips. Even as I made a connection in my brain when the pair's eyes met I'd missed all along and now understood so completely it left me speechless. For happy reasons. Did they know? They must have, were keeping it to themselves. But the love between them was so clear to me in that instant, I wanted to hug them.

Not just best friends then. Soul mates. How had I not seen it before?

Calliope's good humor didn't wane. "Can't we have both?"

Thalia finally laughed, hugged her. While I wanted to tell them they could have it all.

CHAPTER NINE

I let the girls go on ahead, pausing a moment to send Cherise a quick text message filling her in on what I'd seen of Shea's conversation. Thin, yes, but a thread I knew my sheriff friend would pull until the whole blanket of lies fell apart.

The trouble was, by the time I hit send and looked up, they'd both disappeared, the darling pair I adored so much vanished into the interior of the house. I considered texting Calliope to see if she'd point me in the right direction and, instead, shrugged and headed for the corridor behind the staircase, choosing to go right down yet another towering, wide hallway filled with old paintings and stillness.

I paused next to a pair of double doors, peeking inside to find I'd uncovered the location of the library, the sheer size and contents taking me a moment to comprehend. I stepped inside, looking up at the two stories of stories (no pun intended), the dark stained shelves and arched partitions for each shelving section as beautiful as the collection of books hidden away from the world. Who knew what treasures lay there, unseen, unread, hoarded by a wealthy man who could never possibly have the time to read them all?

In case you missed it, I rather loved books. I found myself so entranced, I had crossed to the large table in the center of the room, scent of paper and that distinctive aroma that came with old tomes filling the space despite the volume of air before I realized I wasn't alone.

Gaines's smile had a whimsy to it, an admiration so blatant I caught myself blushing before I took whatever it was going on inside me firmly in hand and reined it in. After all, I'd seen the man behind the charm, enough of him, at least, to be wary of trusting him completely. And while he'd reassured me without knowing it by putting Thalia's interests in their proper place, there was very little else, I was certain, about Gaines Vesterville I could count on.

Of course, the fifteen-year difference in ages had me just as uncomfortable in my admiration of him as anything else. Not that there was something wrong with dating younger or older. For other people, that was.

"Welcome to the library," he said, spreading his arms wide. He'd shed his dress jacket at some point, rolled the sleeves of his white button-up to the forearms, probably the single most delicious thing a man could do to a dress shirt, in my opinion, tan showing against the crisp white, before he tucked his hands into his pockets, smiling down at me as I joined him. Just to show myself I was in control of this situation, thank you, and more than comfortable in his presence.

Wanting to smell him again didn't have anything to do with it, I swear.

Gaines's long, dark lashes blinked slowly over his intense blue eyes, a deeper color than Thalia's, that rich depth of tone that had me turning away so I didn't get lost in them. I had to fight the urge to raise one hand and press it to his chest, crossing my arms over my own to control their activities. I was not going to touch him.

Was *not*.

When I looked away, my gaze settled on a line of photographs on one of the shelves, stacked with what looked like, instead of books, memorabilia of some kind. Curiosity raised, I walked closer, Gaines following me, staying near enough I could feel the warmth radiating from him, a mix of flustered, flattered and slightly alarmed as I did my best to hide the physical reaction I was having to him.

Seriously, the man needed to back off before I did something I'd regret. After I'd done it, not during. Yum.

"My grandfather was in WWII," Gaines said while my gaze skimmed the black and white photos of men in full battle attire, airplanes and one of two men and a woman all seated for a portrait in their dress uniforms.

Why did she look familiar? It took me a moment—I blamed Gaines's proximity—to realize who she reminded me of before blurting, "Eleanor."

Gaines chuckled, the most delicious sound I'd ever heard. I couldn't help myself, looked up at him, turning toward him as he, thankfully, stared at the photo himself with a rueful smile on his face. "You have an excellent eye for detail," he said. "That's Abigail Selling, Eleanor's grandmother. She was in the war with Grandfather." He looked down at me again, smile tightening, voice dropping for dramatic impact. "She was a spy for the Allies, a very successful one."

"Really?" Handsome and yumtastic or not,

that caught my attention and I found myself staring at the smiling woman seated between two men, her confidence in her posture and the way she seemed so comfortable in their midst. "How fascinating."

"She was one of a kind," Gaines said, his tone changing to genuine affection. "I adored her. Grew up listening to her stories." His attention remained on the photo, sharing in an intimate connection as he shifted slightly toward me pointing out details. "That's Grandfather, one of their buddies, Jacob Mitchem. And Abigail."

"Were they...?" I didn't say the word, though I know my implication hit home because Gaines grinned.

"During the war, probably," he said. "Abigail wasn't exactly the Vesterville ideal, however. She had a mind of her own and a way of being that no one could tame." Clearly, he'd adored her as a boy. "She lived here for years after her own husband passed, raised her daughter here, lost her in childbirth when Eleanor was born." More Vesterville tragedy. "Father tolerated her, but Grandfather insisted, wrote it into the will. That's how Eleanor met Chairman, why they married, Grandfather doing his best to honor Abigail. Like most mistakes, it started with good intentions."

Gaines's entire being shifted to slightly bitter, darkness creeping in. "Abby would be so ashamed of what we've become."

"Can I ask you a question?" Gaines nodded, that mercurial shifting from emotion to emotion flickering back to charismatic openness again. "Why do you think your father married Shea?"

He laughed at that, a startled sound, before shaking his head. "You tell me, Seph. You're the therapist." He didn't wait for me to comply, sighing deeply, pulling out his own key from his pocket to examine it. "Who knew why the old man did the things he did?" That sounded rather melancholy though with a hint of humor to it. "As long as he was happy in his last days, does it matter?" When he met my eyes again, his had narrowed, big hand fisting around the gold key with the blue tag dangling between his fingers. "Unless you think she's involved in something nefarious?"

I shrugged, not quite sure what to say, countered with another question instead. "This whole treasure hunt seems rather unusual," I said, to say the least. "Was he…?" Another sentence I didn't finish and didn't have to.

Gaines's handsome face settled into patient kindness, tall body relaxed, radiating focused attention without making me uncomfortable.

He really knew how to play people, didn't he? Where he'd learned it and what defense mechanism it hid I could only guess, but it had to have a lot to do with the family and the fact that, as the youngest son—now the only one until the baby was born, though I had no idea its gender—he likely had a rough go of it in an old and archaic system like this one.

How much of himself had he lost over the years just trying to protect himself from his own family?

"Oh, I beg your pardon." I turned in surprise, Gaines as well, to find Albert had huffed his way into the room. I should have noticed his footfalls and realized just how deeply focused I'd been on Gaines the whole time. To the point, I took a firm and decisive step back, to which he flashed me a sad grin but didn't comment.

"All good, Cousin Albert, old chap," Gaines said, sounding more like he belonged in this house when his grandfather was alive than now. "As far as I can tell, there's nothing to be found here. Have at it." He nodded to me. "Happy hunting." And strode from the room at a casual but ground-eating pace that took him out of sight so fast I couldn't come up with an excuse to follow him.

CHAPTER TEN

Albert had stepped aside to let Gaines leave, now staring at me with hesitation. I smiled reflexively, hoping to put him at ease. Unlike the rest of the Vestervilles, he felt more like a rabbit on the edge of a clearing waiting for a predator to make itself known, another tragic byproduct, clearly, of the family dynamic. How hard had it been to be a mere cousin, on the outside looking into the wealth and prestige? Sure, Gaines had to have had a tough life with two older brothers and all that oppression weighing on him, but at least he bore the name. What punishment and intentional abuse did Albert endure living on the periphery of the Vesterville label?

"No luck yet?" I wasn't sure what response to expect, but when he didn't smile in return, just stood there, I sighed internally and accepted that regardless of his standing, he knew I had less and that was Albert's only concern.

What a mess this family was.

"I'll leave you to it." I tried not to hurry, keeping my pace firm and confident, waiting until I exited to the corridor to finally text Calliope in the hope of catching up with her and Thalia. Because I was done wandering this place on my own. Obviously, I couldn't be trusted without supervision.

Trouble was, my daughter chose not to respond—or, more likely, didn't know I was texting, though her phone was glued to her hand, so the fact she missed my message had me suspecting the first scenario instead of trusting the second was true. That meant my lonely wandering continued, though I made it only a little further down the corridor to the next door before I paused to look inside and found another Vesterville searching for treasure.

This time, however, it was Eleanor who rather heartlessly tossed aside cushions and moved vases without replacing them, even checking the fireplace that dominated the large parlor while I hesitated at the doorway, not sure how to interrupt. Hating the feeling of intrusion that whispered weakness in my mind when it was no such thing.

She finally exhaled a frustrated sigh, spinning to find me standing there, her attempt at a frown only reaching her clenched hands at her sides, far too much going on under her thin skin to control her face's ability to display such contortions. "Yes?" She tsked softly. "If you have to be here, at least don't lurk. It's hideous."

"I take it you haven't found anything yet." You know, I was actually grateful for her cruel rudeness. It snapped me into therapy mode. You'd be surprised how many of my clients start out so angry they are almost impossible to reach. Only calm presence and an unwillingness to allow them the battle they expect settles things. You can't win a war if only one side shows up.

Eleanor tossed her hands, clearly frustrated. "This is ridiculous."

"I didn't realize your father-in-law had this sort of sense of humor." I reached for empathy, let her see it in me, felt her soften just a little.

"My father-in-law," she ground between clenched teeth, "was losing his marbles at the end, apparently." She shook off the show of anger before settling back into disdainful composure. "Regardless of this asinine little game he decided to play on us, I'll be contesting the results."

"You think he wasn't in his right mind?" I was wondering the same thing, frankly.

Eleanor barked a sharp and furious laugh. "I think Reginald Vesterville was a nasty and abusive old man who loved to stir us against one another and cause as much suffering as possible while he laughed at us."

Tell me how you really feel, El. "I'm sorry," I said. "It couldn't have been easy. Was it hard growing up here?" She seemed surprised by that question. "I heard about your grandmother, Abigail. She sounded amazing."

Eleanor had tensed for some reason, closing off from me instead of opening up, which meant either she had less of a happy history with the supposed spy in the family than Gaines or she had something to hide. Made me want to know which.

"If you don't mind," she snapped, "I have a nonsensically preposterous task ahead of me before I can finally bury my husband." She left the room, striding past me and I let her go. Whatever I'd triggered in her, she ran from it as clearly as she ran from her feelings.

I'd feel sorry for all of them if I wasn't starting to think they all deserved one another.

What I wasn't expecting? For Lloyd to enter the parlor, quietly closing the door behind him with his pristine, white-gloved hands before he turned to me, frown of anxiety on his long, lean face.

"Ms. Pringle," he said. "You were asking about Ms. Abigail." I nodded. "Did I hear the sheriff mention cyanide?"

Okay, what was this, then? And what did the two things have in common that had Lloyd so obviously concerned? I nodded once more, staying silent and letting him work out his internal conflict while he shifted in visible discomfort, frowning at the floor before looking up again, face set in sorrowful decision.

"In that case," he said, "there's something you need to see."

I followed him as he led me to the far end of the corridor, up a hidden set of stairs without the fancy wood paneling, a servant's means of reaching the other floors behind a door disguised as a wall. Made me wonder how many secrets this old mansion held, even as we passed the third floor and stopped at a narrow doorway at the top.

Lloyd finally spoke as he stepped through, flicking on a light switch, the vast dimness of what had to be the wing's attic stretching out before us.

"This way, Ms. Pringle," he said. "I think you may find this of particular interest."

Maybe I should have been nervous to follow the butler into the gloom despite the overhead bulbs. It was obvious to me no one in the family frequented the creepy place, packed with what seemed like endless antiques, boxes, wardrobes and a multitude of household items that had been replaced or forgotten over the years since the estate came to be. Lloyd, however, seemed quite confident in the contents, weaving his way through what amounted to corridors between stacks of items until he paused near a corner. We had to be over the residences, though I'd lost track of my space/time positioning, I had to admit.

I took a moment to scan the small selection he'd brought to my attention, a woman's WWII uniform on a mannequin, pinned with metals and strangely free of dust despite the layer of it on a few of the boxes and one dresser nearby. It was easy enough to identify the subject of a tall painting of who could only be Abigail Selling behind the dress form, her smile as enigmatic and liberated as the one in the photo in the library and just as clear of the passing of time's layers as the jacket she'd once worn with so much pride.

None of which seemed to be Lloyd's reason

for bringing me here. Instead, he gestured to a particular piece of history. Amid a small collection of boxes and a tall wardrobe, sat a heavy steamer trunk that had seen war, no doubt about it, A.S. pressed into a bronze placard screwed to the top.

"This was Abigail's," I said, crouching to look, marveling despite myself at the unique piece, wondering what it had seen along her journeys.

"Yes, ma'am," Lloyd said. "What remains of her possessions have been here since she passed since Ms. Eleanor had no use for them." Was he judging her? If so, he didn't show it or come across that way. "When Ms. Eleanor expressed a desire to discard them, Mr. Reginald had all of Ms. Abigail's things put in storage when she left us in case Ms. Eleanor changed her mind." Now his tone altered, sorrow emerging, old grief, but for Abigail's death or Eleanor's lack of care I wasn't sure. "You may want to take a closer look at the contents."

I looked up at him, squinting into the dust motes and dimness, wondering at his propensity for mystery at a time like this. Protecting the family, perhaps? He seemed uncomfortable with the whole thing, enough I had to believe his actions went against some kind of honor code he alone bore. Trust me, the family wouldn't have shown a scrap of such loyalty to him. "Lloyd," I said. "You mind telling me what you think I'm going to find?"

He hesitated, pursed his lips, quickly shook his head and stared at the floor, silent and waiting. He'd done as much as he was willing, or his integrity would allow.

Which had my curiosity all the more piqued. The trunk wasn't locked, to my surprise, as shocking as the contents. While I'd never seen old school spy craft items before, it was pretty clear to me the kit I looked down into, from the biscuit tin that, when the lid was opened, revealed a radio inside, to what looked like an ordinary pipe but, at closer inspection, had a barrel and space for bullets instead of tobacco. A stack of documents tucked neatly into a wooden box claimed Abigail Selling—or her likeness, at least—was also Fraulein Lena Ernst from Berlin, Anna Ivanov from St. Petersburg and many more. But the most fascinating was the small metal box filled with pea-sized capsules filled with crystalline powder. Several of which were missing.

"I believe," Lloyd said quietly while I stared down at what I now guessed was the murder weapon, "you've found what the sheriff is looking for."

CHAPTER ELEVEN

Now, not that I was an expert in cyanide capsules or anything, but even after how many decades tucked away since the war, the scent of bitter almonds was unmistakable. I took a quick picture and sent it off to Cherise before looking up once again, standing while my knees cracked in protest I'd been crouched for so long, to ask Lloyd some obvious questions.

"Does everyone have access to the attic?" I had to assume yes, but one never knew. There was such a lack of trust in this place, it was possible Lloyd was in charge of keys or something of that nature. Though, he'd simply opened the door when we arrived, so that seemed unlikely at this point.

"Of course," he said, dashing my hope perhaps there was a restricted list. "This part of the attic contains the family's possessions. It's never locked, though rarely do any of them request anything from here."

"So, they don't come up here themselves?" Right, why would they when they had servants to do their bidding?

Lloyd hesitated, then shook his head. "Madam, I can't say for certain." He gestured at the floor that seemed clean despite the dust on some of the items, like Abigail's uniform. "I am surprised to find, however, someone took time to remove the dust from this area."

"Hiding their tracks," I said. But why bother clearing it from the uniform and painting? Maybe whoever had come up here decided to make it look like the whole area had been recently cleaned to throw off suspicions. Which led me to my second question.

"And how about the trunk," I said. "Who knows about it and what's in it?"

"Ms. Eleanor," he said very firmly, then blanched, lined face tightening before he relented, sorrow returning. "Her grandmother gifted it to her on her deathbed." Like he was there or something. Which he must have been to sound so sure of himself. "Despite the fact her most prized possession, the music box she cherished and promised Ms. Eleanor, was missing." He stopped, stared into my eyes, licked his lips. Debating he'd said more than he meant to? Then shrugged, all in. "Ms. Eleanor was most disappointed in the loss. *Most* disappointed."

In other words, she threw a fit while her grandmother lay dying. Classy.

"Anyone else?" He'd left the suspect pool wide open with his admission anyone could make their way to the attic at any time, though pointing fingers at Eleanor did seem to be the first place to start. And led me to believe Lloyd, despite his loyalty to the family, suspected Chairman's wife of murder.

He knew them far better than I did. And it certainly fit if the cyanide that killed her husband matched the contents of her grandmother's spy kit.

Lloyd carried on now without pause as though he'd come to peaceful terms with his decision to call her out, that sadness crossing his face again. "I can only assume the whole family knew," he said. "Ms. Abigail loved to tell stories of her days in the war and after. The trunk's existence is hardly a secret. Nor was her job."

Gaines said as much in the library. So, everyone knew exactly what Abigail was up to. But did they know she kept a deadly poison on the premises as a reminder of who she used to be?

My phone chimed and I checked the text, confirming Cherise and not my absent daughter finally getting back to me or anything. *Tell me you didn't touch it.*

Whoops. *Sorry, I didn't know what it was.* Immediately guilt I'd tampered with evidence was squashed with her hurried reply.

Not your fault. Bag it if you can, leave it if you can't. I'm on my way.

Anything back from the lab? I knew it was too soon but had to ask.

Not yet, she sent, *though Owen ran a second test when I asked. Definitely cyanide. I did find something interesting. Turns out Shea's background? Shallow. Like, fake ID shallow.*

Huh. *So she's hiding a past,* I sent. *That doesn't make her a murderer.*

Or it does and she's done something like this before. Cherise's big city homicide detective influence was showing, her tendency to think the worst of people flaring up when she was working. I understood completely and had to admit I jumped to the same conclusion. *Just hang on to the evidence so no one can tamper with it, and I'll take it from there.*

I turned to Lloyd. "Can I get a plastic bag?"

He instantly turned and headed for a cabinet, opening the drawer, returning with a fresh bag like he'd known what I was going to ask for. "We wrap many of the items before we store them," he said.

Perfect for me. I gingerly tipped the box with the capsules into the bag and sealed it with the zipper top, taking it with me when I stood and gestured for Lloyd to lead us out. Because no way was I finding my way in yet another maze, grateful he stuck it out to guide me.

He paused at the hall, hesitating before holding out his hand. "I assume you'll continue your observation of the events unfolding?" I nodded. "Perhaps you would trust me with the evidence to deliver to the sheriff personally?" He sounded like it mattered a lot to him, pale eyes sad, so sad, rimmed with tears. "I desire very much to bring the murderer to justice in some small way, Ms. Pringle. Is it permitted?"

I almost turned him down, but instead found myself depositing the bag and contents into his hands. He tucked it against his chest and nodded slowly before walking away while I hoped I hadn't just made a terrible mistake.

On the other hand, he not only guided me right to the murder weapon, something he could have disposed of quietly without alerting anyone if he really wanted it covered up, he seemed like the only person in the house I could trust. And carrying cyanide capsules around in full sight of the others would raise questions I'd rather not answer without Cherise to handle them for me.

Which meant we parted ways when I reached the main hall, heading for the foyer as my phone vibrated again. I paused to check it, Calliope's message unread as the sound of voices caught my attention and pulled my focus up to a shadowy corner under the stairs.

Where Albert had just grabbed Eleanor's arm, tugged her to him and kissed her with enough passion I figured it wasn't the first time. She kissed him briefly, confirming my gut instinct from the key ceremony, the tenderness with which he looked at her and raised such a suggestion long before this proof presented itself. Instead of lingering, she then pushed him away and marched past him, heading in the other direction. Thankfully. I wasn't sure I wanted the two of them to know I'd seen that they both had motive for murder.

I sent a quick text to Cherise while feeling a bit like a voyeur or a paparazzo spying on celebrities for dirt and money, shaking off the guilt of it by reminding myself someone in this house killed Chairman Vesterville and that had to be more important than the privacy of two people for whom infidelity could have been the reason the eldest son died not so long ago.

I debated my next move when the text I'd received wasn't from Calliope after all, but a client looking to book an appointment, debating waiting for Cherise in the foyer or continuing my hunt for information while the others followed the old man's crazy plan. Until the sound of someone shouting had me running before I could stop myself, skidding to a halt in the library of all places, where Gaines stood, grinning, arm around Shea's shoulders, the young woman clearly furious he'd caught her with the prize, while the pregnant widow cradled a small, black painted box in both hands.

I wasn't the only one who'd heard him call out, because a moment later Eleanor pushed her way past me, Albert a bit more gentlemanly, the girls joining in a rush from wherever it was they'd been searching. I frowned at my daughter's clear delight at the find, though she refused to retreat to contrite, winking at me instead.

"Our clever step-mummy made the first discovery," Gaines said at his most cheerfully irritating while she jerked herself free of his embrace, clutching the box to her chest. "Apparently, Seph and I were looking in the right place, but failed to investigate fully." He pointed at the photo we'd been examining,

Abigail Selling no longer smiling from the shelf, her frame tipped on its face. "The old man thought she was an excellent protector of the first box, but even Abigail couldn't stand against your cleverness, could she, my dear?" That he aimed at the pregnant woman who had tucked her body around the box as if he planned to snatch it from her.

"I found it," Shea snarled more akin to a cornered badger ready for a fight than a delicate young woman in the family way. "It's *mine*."

"It actually belongs to whoever has the key that fits it, my dear," Gaines corrected her. "Shall we find out?" So much challenge in that question, in the almost maniacal smile he fixed her with as though daring her to try to stop his father's last wish from being fulfilled.

She finally tsked, pulling out her key from her bosom, a rather unconventional hiding place for a lady if Eleanor's eye roll and exasperated sigh judged it. Shea ignored her, jamming the key into the box's lock, exposing the Vesterville crest on the top.

"Now we know what to look for," Calliope whispered to Thalia. My child needed a lesson in manners.

After a few seconds of grunting and more swearing I won't repeat here because that sort of thing was really unnecessary, Shea finally relented, jerking her key free and practically throwing the box at Gaines before storming from the room, red-faced and furious.

"A shame," he said, mocking her as she exited. "But an opportunity, nonetheless, for another of our esteemed gathering. Ladies first?" He offered the box to Eleanor who joined him with a suspicious expression as she retrieved her key from the pocket of her light blue suit's skirt—lucky her, pockets in a skirt—and tried the lock. To no avail. But when Gaines reached for it, she brushed him off.

"I have one more to try," she said. Replaced her own and reached into the other pocket for the second, the black and silver key that had been Chairman's glinting dully.

Again she failed, however, the key merely jamming in the mechanism. She finally handed it over, resentment in her face, Gaines turning to Thalia while Albert, in a rare show of spine, stepped into Eleanor's place and took possession. Gaines seemed as surprised as the rest of them, nodded to his cousin without a requisite smartass remark, let the trembling financial manager have his go.

The moment he inserted his key I had a feeling and, when it turned smoothly, clicking like the last tick of a clock or the end of a heartbeat, the anticipation hit all of us at once, the entire room falling silent while I'm positive I wasn't the only one who held my breath.

As Albert's shaking fingers released the key. Touched the lid.

And opened the box.

CHAPTER TWELVE

I wasn't sure what I was expecting, though the resulting moment of nothing felt a bit like a letdown. It wasn't like the box was going to leap up and bite him or anything, or something within trumpet its intent, expel some poisonous gas, shoot off fireworks, yada yada, fanfare and mayhem. The anticlimax lingered regardless, while Albert reached inside and pulled out, not gold or jewels or a smoking gun, but just another letter.

I really was becoming jaded, and I had the Vestervillians to thank.

This time it was only a folded-over page, not even encased in an envelope for that satisfying reveal from the shroud of expensive stationery. Reginald had either lost his interest in the show or simply wanted to downplay the importance of those he'd sent on this wild goose chase. Mind you, the page had been sealed with the same black wax and Vesterville stamp, so there was that much pomp and ceremony attached, feeling less official and more mocking to me. Yes, I might have been overplaying it in my mind, weaving a narrative that had nothing to do with Reginald's intent, but I couldn't help but assess and weigh every choice against his need to punish his family for whatever reason he deemed necessary.

The young driver, Fielder Grant, had been right. No love lost here.

There was one item of note, at least, that added a moment of curiosity and breathless anticipation I should have been immune to but found myself leaning toward despite myself. A small key slid into Albert's palm when he tipped the box over to retrieve the last item inside, the ordinary enough looking item a far cry from the elaborate ones Reginald contrived for the container he'd used to hide this new clue.

Gaines took the box from Albert without hesitation, examining it quickly before setting it aside as Albert read the front of the folded page.

"'For Albert,'" he said. "'To receive your due, this must be read aloud in the company of all keyholders.'"

That meant fetching Shea. But, as I turned to do so, I realized she'd never actually left, the sullen young widow lurking at the doorway, Albert noting her presence before he broke the seal and unfolded the page, reading in a voice that cracked before smoothing out.

"'I've known of your affair with Eleanor for many years.'" Albert stuttered to a halt, paling, then flushing red, looking up at her as he stopped, shaking his head while she muttered something in clear disgust and waved at him.

"Just read it," she snapped. "No one cares anymore, Albert."

He swallowed so hard his Adam's apple lurched then resumed in a quieter voice that gained some strength but never returned to full volume as though he feared what else might be revealed. Like murder? "'However, despite your dalliances, you are still family and, for that reason alone, I relent.'" Albert wiped at his upper lip, sheen of sweat beading his forehead as he went on. "'Venture now to Chairman's office where you must unlock the bottom drawer of my eldest son's desk and uncover what is hidden there.'" He looked up from the page, flipped it over, glanced at the empty back, shrugged. "That's it." Another look at Eleanor, longing and terror intermingled, was cut short by a firm clap on the back courtesy of Gaines who might have been smiling and jovial on the outside, but whose blow sent Albert staggering just a little.

"You heard the old man," the youngest Vesterville brother said. "Let's see what Chairman thought was worth locking away from the rest of us."

I stepped back, let the others go ahead of me, trailing after the girls, mind whirling. What would Chairman have done if he was still alive, and his secrets were about to be revealed? Was that perhaps part of the reason he was killed, to prevent him from letting the truth out? Or, more likely, was the truth itself the source of his death's motivation?

Okay, now I was invested. And fought off the thrill I knew that had my daughter so enthusiastically engaged despite everything.

I had just entered when Albert pulled the drawer to Chairman's desk open, the darkly oppressive room a cookie-cutter to the rest of the house, aside from the tall and tyrannical portrait of him that glared at me in silent recrimination as I entered. I ignored him in favor of the financial manager who retrieved a large manila envelope from the drawer and set it on the desk before using Chairman's own letter opener to part the flap.

One look at the contents had Albert spluttering all over again, this time his outrage and anxiety turning to anger. "This is… what was he thinking?" He looked up, meeting Eleanor's eyes, extending the pages to her. "He was going to betray us all."

She snatched them, scanned them, her fury a whiplash of heated expletives that could have taught Shea a thing or two about swearwords.

But it was Gaines who grimly read over her shoulder, who informed the rest of us what the paperwork contained. "Looks like dear Chairman decided he wanted another lawyer or two," he said. "Cutting you out completely, sister dearest." She snarled at him, but he went on like she hadn't reacted. "And that he planned, once Father died, to make sure his will cut everyone out of the inheritance, divorce and kick us all to the proverbial curb." He looked up then, smiled that viper smile at the young woman carrying the newest Vesterville. "All but Shea." Gaines's tone didn't change while Eleanor glared at her in utter rage, unable to speak, just vibrating in that hate she held so deeply while her brother-in-law went on. "Now, what would motivate Chairman to such charity, I wonder, dear step-mummy for his own father's widow and the heir to the family's fortune?"

Albert pulled another sheet of paper from the envelope, so pale now he looked like he might pass out at any moment. "Because," he said, "according to this paternity test, the baby isn't Reginald's." He finally found his classic Vestervillian arrogance and accusatory tone. "It was Chairman's."

Now, in the light of what had been revealed, I expected an outburst of some kind. Shouting, name-calling, more swearing that would burn the ears of the most jaded. What I hadn't planned on? Eleanor practically leaping the desk to attack Shea with a guttural shriek that sounded far more animal than human.

If it hadn't been for Thalia, I was pretty sure the two widows would have torn one another apart. As it stood, the brave young woman I adored instead put herself into the line of fire and managed to wrangle her aunt before she could choke the life out of her step-grandmother. Who happened to be carrying her cousin.

Yikes.

Gaines started to laugh, drawing focus, even cutting through Eleanor's continuing attempts to reach Shea while I joined Thalia and Calliope in putting distance between the two women. His genuine humor, a deep and almost infectious laugh that came from the depths of him as he slapped one thigh with his empty hand, the other holding the paperwork still, had an oddly alluring quality that I had to fight not to join into. Gaines finally subsided, though he continued to chuckle to himself as he looked around to the rest of the family, even meeting my eyes once with authentic amusement before he spoke at last.

"Only the Vestervilles," he said.

No one spoke for a long time. While my mind asked the question that had to be asked—was Chairman the target after all? And, more importantly...

"I wonder what's in the other boxes," Gaines said, cobalt eyes twinkling. While the rest of the gathering froze. Then split apart and ran for the door, the hunt for the rest of Reginald's cruel joke driving them out including my daughter and Thalia, though they looked excited now, both of them, not just Calliope. And I had a feeling I knew why though if Reginald kept the identity of her parent's murderer to himself and was only willing to tell her after she earned it.

Yeah. Vestervilles.

Gross.

Only two people remained, Gaines again clapping a hand on Albert's shoulder, while the cousin glared into the drawer, then up at the man beside him, face set and sullenly petulant.

"That's it?" He looked near to tears. "Where's my inheritance?"

Gaines's smile never wavered. "I guess the old man thought Eleanor was enough of a hand-me-down." He laughed, strolled out, winking at me as he did, while Albert's fury and ineffective impotence traveled through his shaking body in a visible wave of hurt that had to be tearing him to pieces on the inside. But, before I could offer comfort or a chance to talk, he ran from the room, leaving me to sigh and hope Cherise arrived soon before this family imploded on their multitude of secrets.

I'd had enough of the Vestervilles—all but Thalia, that was—to last me a lifetime.

CHAPTER THIRTEEN

As I emerged from Chairman's office at last, I noticed Shea perched on one of the seats next to the door, answering my earlier question if anyone actually used them or not to the affirmative. Though this was Shea, an interloper, we were talking about, so it was even more probably a massive faux pas.

Especially since, instead of the retiring and placid pregnant widow lost in her melancholy, she instead madly typed into her phone with her brows and nose scrunching in concentration, scowling at the screen while she composed her message before hitting the send button and sighing in a heaving expression of dissatisfaction. Looked up and found me yet again watching her.

Ah, there was the guilty flicker of someone

doing something she really shouldn't have been up to at a time like this. But what exactly might that something be, I wondered?

"What do you want this time?" She seemed out of steam despite her sharp words and tone, far more petulant and toddler sulky than imperious, sinking into the cushions of the large antique, wide arms really too broad a width for her, looking small and almost juvenile on the substantial piece of furniture.

A little girl having a baby. Poor thing. And yes, I meant the unborn child.

"You must have known Chairman planned to cut everyone out," I said. Forget preamble at this point. If she was going to be nasty, I'd hold my temper in light of her condition but not pull any punches. She came into this eyes wide open, didn't she? Likely planned on seducing Chairman from day one, had it all laid out to take advantage of the childless heir while fooling the old man into giving her everything she wanted.

Sucked that didn't exactly work out. And yes, I was a terrible person for giggle snorting over it, but I kept that on the inside, so it didn't count, right?

I needed to get out of this house. I was losing my ability to care about others.

Shea made an unhappy face, glancing down

the hallway toward where the sound of the others talking—at least they were talking now—told us they were otherwise occupied. "I knew," she said. Tilted her chin down, met my eyes with her dark ones, fluttering her thick lashes. "But he loved me, not Eleanor. He knew about her affair. I didn't mean to fall in love with him, too. It's just, Reggie was so old and couldn't satisfy me the way Chairman did."

I snorted, couldn't help myself, while Shea flapped a hand at me as her expression shifted to irritation from that mocking attempt at a lie. "I just bet," I said.

She sat up a little straighter, rubbing her baby bump with a tired exhale. "Listen," she said, "I don't know what horse you have in this race aside from Thalia, but I'll tell you one thing. They are messed up, the whole lot of them, and none of them deserve a dime." Shea glanced at her phone as it buzzed. "Now, if you'll excuse me, thanks to Chairman's death and this ridiculous will, I have to sing for my supper. Again." Like the baby she bore was a burden she had to endure to get the money she thought she was owed. I let her go, only because I was sure she had no reason to kill Chairman and in fact, his death had so ruined her plans for an easy life she'd likely put an end to whoever *did* murder her meal ticket.

One down, the rest of these crazy people—again, Thalia notwithstanding—to go. That was unless Cherise found someone on staff or with access to the house who did it in which case, I was merely poking my nose into the sordid and truly wretched lives and affairs—literally—of the Vestervilles.

Lucky me.

Which had me thinking and turned me around. I headed to Chairman's desk, flipped through the discarded pages Gaines left behind, the paternity test Albert fished out of the envelope last. Noted the sticky with *I knew it was her fault all along!* in bold black marker attached. So, he blamed Eleanor for their lack of progeny? Was it a bone of contention? It had to be, and likely Eleanor had tried to blame him. But if he managed to impregnate Shea, that meant Chairman was right and his widow was the fertility issue.

Using "Chairman" and "right" in the same sentence made me gag a little.

The will draft he'd had drawn up seemed straightforward enough, no mention whatsoever of any of the family, only he and Shea and their unborn child. That meant exactly what it looked like. Aside from whatever money they already possessed, Chairman had poised himself to take control of the estate. Did he have any idea his father had other plans? I could only imagine he'd been told or led to believe he was to inherit the bulk of the family fortune. The last page even outlined, in his handwriting, his plan to contest the will he assumed was to be read today, all the things he intended to use to declare his father incompetent, including his marriage to a woman a third his age.

Despicable? Yes. Dead? No wonder.

And my intolerance for asshattery was showing. Whoops.

I tugged on the drawer, opening it all the way. Noticed a business card in the back, pulled it out. The plain, black card read, *Personal Cleaning Service* and, on the reverse, a number.

That was it. All kinds of weird. Which meant, naturally, I had to call it, right? Sure, it could have been just a stray something Chairman discarded that accidentally ended up in the drawer. It may not have had anything at all to do with anything. After all, what did someone like him have to do with cleaning? The man had servants for that. But something about the wording, the deeply etched block numbers in black ink on the back, the heavy thickness of the paper and plain black and white had my curiosity—and intuition—fired up enough I took a chance and hit send.

All while anxiously biting my thumb nail as I debated the brilliance of my decision. Almost hung up twice, held on, both to my courage and my breath, until the line clicked, and I exhaled slowly in response to the voice on the other end.

"Thank you for contacting us with your cleaning needs. Price list upon request. Please state the nature of your cleaning requirements or ask for a quote on multiple services. Leave your number and we'll get back to you." The message ended and, before I could stop myself, I squeaked, "Price list, please!" Then read out my area code and cell number and hung up.

While realizing I'd just given my contact information to someone or some organization of shadowy origins and may just have made a huge mistake I'd be regretting in short order.

Eep.

Except, there really was no solid reason to be nervous, I reasoned, sliding the card into my pocket. No, no solid reason. So why then did I have a feeling "cleaning" was a code for something far more sinister than I was willing to admit yet and if Chairman was involved with said cleaning, there was more than likely a contemptible and possible loathsome reason for him to have said card in his possession and...

Well, too late now. One way or another, relevant or not, no stone unturned and all that, right?

You know that feeling you get when you're being watched? That raised the hair on your arms, goosebumpy feeling that had you looking over your shoulder? I didn't have to do much more than glance up, Gaines standing in the doorway, that sexy smile of his making me nervous now instead of worked up.

Except, of course, for the black box he held in one hand that drove me to my feet.

He chuckled at my excited reaction. "Hey, beautiful," he said. "Want to see what's in it?"

CHAPTER FOURTEEN

Let's just skim over the fact Gaines called me beautiful and get to the good part because I know you know I was well aware he was teasing me as much as he taunted and tormented the rest of the family. Likely couldn't help himself.

Still. Captain Gorgeouspants called fifty-year-old and sometimes self-critical of age and weight and time flying me *beautiful*.

Ahem.

Instead, I invite you to rejoin the rest of the family as Gaines called them into the parlor this time, Eleanor seemingly unhappy to find I was the first one there, Shea and the girls entering a moment later. I almost mentioned Albert. Would he even join us? Except, I suppose his curiosity and hope outweighed his bitter disappointment so deeply embedded in his face and posture that he couldn't help himself, slumping his way into our presence last.

"Another of Father's delights," Gaines said in that smooth voice of his, displaying it on his open palm. He turned to me, handed me his key. "Found under his bed, of all places. I guess he ran out of cleverness, in the end, to decide on such a mundane hiding place. Or maybe it was a suggestion, do you think?" Blue eyes settled on me, the implication in his tone so powerful I was sure everyone heard it. "In light of Father's penchant for the romantic, would you do the honors of trying mine for me, please, lovely Seph?"

He had to stop doing this to me. Either that or I had to find a way to keep him from influencing me. I took the key, warm from his pocket, and did the deed, shaking my head as it stuck partway before handing it back. His fake sad face moue ended with a grin as he looked up and those stunning eyes shifted from me, and I could breathe again.

"Eleanor," he said. "Would you like a go?"

She didn't have to shove me aside, I'd already moved out of the way, though when her key failed to turn the lock and her frustrated snarl led her to pull out the silver and black meant for Chairman, it was Shea who added to her angst with a cruel interruption.

"That key should be in my hands," the pregnant girl said with about as much bold bluster as I'd ever heard from anyone. Brave soul, though she didn't seem to realize she'd tempted Eleanor to attack her again, the fellow widow fisting the key as if to protect it or, even, use it as a weapon.

"Over my dead body," Eleanor rasped.

"Please, dear sister," Gaines said at his most mocking. "Don't tempt fate."

She smacked him firmly before fixing Shea with her vicious glare. "He was my husband when he died," she said. "You don't have him yet." And now, never would.

Shea looked like she wanted to argue, jaw jutting, until her phone buzzed. She glanced at the screen, froze a second, then shrugged. "Fine," she said. "Get on with it."

Eleanor unfolded her fingers like it hurt. Jammed the key into the lock and turned it smoothly. Her surprise it worked only lasted a moment, the top yielding to her free hand, key left behind as she cracked the seal on the letter and read it out loud as Albert had done.

"'I am well aware of what you have planned, my boy, and I've taken firm steps to ensure none of it comes to pass.'" Wait, did that mean… did Reginald plan on Chairman's murder before he died? Was his eldest son's death as contrived as the rest of this? "'While you've believed all along the bulk of the Vesterville fortune will be yours, I've had second thoughts as of late and this is the result.'" Okay, so no. Not even the elderly patriarch had that kind of power, and now I was jumping at shadows that didn't exist. Not to mention the fact the letter was addressed to Chairman for him to read, Persephone. Sheesh, get a grip. "'There was a time perhaps you would have been worthy of all that our family's history has to offer. I command you now, instead, to go to my office and open the locked filing cabinet's top drawer and discover what I've decided you deserve.'"

Eleanor's rage had her balling the page in her hand. Until she looked up suddenly, gleeful ferocity aimed at Shea. She held the crumpled paper toward the pregnant girl who had turned very, very pale. "So much for Chairman's plan." She actually cackled, and I worried his widow had cracked down the middle under the pressure of all this. "Reginald knew, I bet you anything. About you, the baby." She spoke that last word as half-curse, though filled with longing as she inhaled a wobbly breath, so close to tears I was positive she was going to collapse.

I needn't have worried. Gaines prodded her with that same crap-eating grin he'd been wearing to torture them all. "Shall we find out if you're right?" He tipped the box, a small key dropping into his hand which he offered up to Eleanor.

She snatched it with a soft animal-like moan and ran for the door, the rest of us letting her go before she could knock anyone over in her rush.

I fell in step with Thalia, arm around her shoulders on impulse while Calliope moved a step ahead, keeping her distance but clearly still enraptured by the unfolding events.

"You holding up all right, sweetheart?" I kept my voice low enough no one else would hear, offering as much support and love as I could while we walked toward what could very well be yet another emotionally devastating bomb drop and likely was.

Thalia actually smiled at me. "I really am, Seph," she said. "I'm surprised at myself. I thought it would be harder, but Grandpa Reginald's little game has made it, I don't know. Not fun, by any means."

"Don't tell Callie, that," I said with enough sarcasm Thalia giggled.

"She's adorable, isn't she?" Her pale blue

eyes went to my daughter and back to me again. Was that a flicker of guilt? I hoped not. I just nodded for her to go on. "No, more cathartic. He wasn't the kindest man, Seph. But he was always good to me."

I squeezed her then let her go as we approached a doorway, Eleanor hot-footing through, the others right behind her. "Whatever happens," I said, "you have me and Callie, you know that, right?"

She stopped, took my hands, beamed at me, the sunlight of her smile the best part of Thalia. "I do," she said. "And I'll always be grateful, Seph. Because of you two, I'm not one of them, not really." She sighed, shook her head. "Part of me has never felt like a real Vesterville. And you know what?" She laughed then. "I'm so grateful."

Tell me about it. "Let's go see what your grandfather had in store for Chairman."

We were slow enough on entry, the crime scene tape ignored, returning to the exact place this had all started. Eleanor already had the cabinet door jerked open, contents strewn on the floor until she found what she was looking for. Pulled out a heavy file, slammed it down on the desk, flipped open the top protective sheet and stopped. Face falling utterly still, eyes almost bugging out. Before she started to cackle again, the laughter taking her down, only Albert's proximity and quick movement keeping her from falling to the floor from the sobbing hysteria she let take her over.

While Gaines, a gleefully wicked smile on his face, read the top page. "Turns out Daddy-O had the paternity test redone, dear Shea, dear Mummy." He tossed her the paper which she took, sheet white and now desperately looking around like she expected to be lynched. "So, if Father wasn't the sperm donor and Chairman was firing blanks, as usual, who is the bouncy baby's other half, do tell?"

Oh. Boy.

"You killed him." Eleanor finally managed to get herself to her feet, though far from under control, snarling rage and that edge of hysteria mingling into the kind of emotional turmoil that murder was made of. Except, of course, she wasn't *doing* but *accusing*, right? "You knew Chairman would find out the truth and cut you out, too, so you killed him." She was screaming by now, so I was guessing at some of the words, but her last two she got out fairly clearly. "ADMIT IT!"

Shea sank into a chair, the paper shaking so violently in her hand, her small, pale face vulnerable for the first time to the point I really did worry about the baby. "Chairman didn't know. He believed the fake test I gave him. I had no idea Reggie…" She choked on that, sobbed, dropping the sheet, cupping her full belly with both hands, protective, shielding. "I didn't know Reggie found out the truth. Which means he knew who I really was." She sobbed again, caught it, held it in with visible agony. "This is a scam, okay? I just wanted the money. I swear, I didn't kill anyone."

"Who's the father, Shea?" I had a good idea I already knew but had to check into something first. While she mutely shook her head.

"I want a lawyer." And sank deeper into the seat, now lost in her weeping, while Eleanor shrieked her fury, Albert trying to shush her, Calliope and Thalia standing close to me, Gaines's grin finally getting on my nerves.

CHAPTER FIFTEEN

It took Cherise long enough to show up. I mean, come on, I'd messaged her what felt like a year ago when I was still in the attic, hadn't I? Made it clear she should arrive post-haste and make her official presence known so I could hand over the goods now in Lloyd's possession (what had I been thinking?)? It had been years since that call, hadn't it?

Nope. Apparently, when I checked my phone and the last text she'd sent claiming she was on the way, it turned out only forty-five minutes had ticked by in the timeframe required between finding the cyanide and all the drama that unfolded in between before she strode through the front door again. Still, it was a fifteen-minute drive from the station. What kept her?

I forced an inhale at the sight of her, regained my composure, felt the veil of that place, its attempt to wrangle me under its grim control, attempt to force me into submission fading along with my imagination's wild run thinking this house was capable of anything of the sort.

Still. Time had a weirdness to it in this place I attributed not just to the anxiety and tension heightened to the breaking point at what felt like a constant level. So, I had to give it to the Vestervilles. They didn't do anything halfway, not even morphing the rules of reality to their will.

We'd all exited Reginald's office together as though of one mind about remaining behind where Chairman had already died, where the ashes of the family patriarch stood in stern overwatch on the desk in his black and silver urn. I stayed with Calliope and Thalia, the group breaking off into small bits and pieces, Eleanor visibly irritated that Albert hovered near her though I was sure it was less out of a need to protect her and more to make her a shield of his own. Gaines and Shea were the only two who stood alone, though the pregnant widow at least had her unborn baby to caress over and over for her own comfort. For his part, the youngest brother of the family seemed unfazed and even continually amused by the entire process.

Cherise, however, was not, bless her, the seriousness of her expression, the authority emanating from her more-than-impressive person silencing everyone as she approached in that long, steady stride that owned the foyer despite its massiveness. If anyone could dominate Vesterville House, it was Cherise King.

She'd accepted the plastic bag Lloyd instantly handed over the moment she entered, no pause in her step as she marched past him, only coming to a halt when she was within a few feet of us, grim, towering Amazonian sheriff persona in full reveal as she held up the box I'd bagged for her.

"Anyone want to venture a guess as to what this is?" She didn't offer to let anyone take it in hand, despite the fact Eleanor reached for it herself with a shocked expression of recognition registering.

"That belonged to my grandmother," she said, indignance about all she could muster since her breakdown, her well-sprayed hair now sagging, the dark circles under her eyes accentuated by her weeping and the mascara that pooled in the lines there. "What are you doing with my property?"

Considering Lloyd's story about her lack of interest in her grandmother's possessions, her acquisitive demand seemed rather out of line. Of course, she'd just been through a bit of a wringer, so perhaps it was her only way of buoying herself, one last attempt to retake control in the face of someone she really didn't want to cross without her full faculties in place.

"Your *property*," Cherise said, "happens to be cyanide, Mrs. Vesterville, the very poison that killed your husband." Of course, Cherise had no idea if it was the very poison, though her wording, I knew, had less to do with utter truth and more with carefully timed and placed supposition meant to stir a possible admission of guilt.

"You're saying someone—the killer—used Grandmother's old spy stuff to murder Chairman?" Eleanor's lips trembled, one hand going to her throat in a convulsive grasp, Albert's hand settling on her shoulder before she shrugged it off. "Why would anyone do that?"

"Maybe you'd like to tell me, Mrs. Vesterville," Cherise said. "Since, as you said, this was once Abigail Selling's."

Eleanor spun, jabbed an index finger at Shea. "She's a grifter and a liar and not even pregnant with a Vesterville." That all came out in a string of words without breath or space between them, the still distraught new widow accusing the more seasoned one with a shaking hand and all the resentment and hate she could muster. "You should be looking into her, Sheriff King, not me. I had no reason..." Eleanor trailed off, going so white I was positive she was about to pass out, almost moved, Albert catching her around the waist as she forced a breath. "I had no reason." Eleanor looked around at all of us while the reveals of the last three-quarters of an hour made her a liar. "I didn't!"

"Let's see, dear sister," Gaines said with a cheery grin, ticking off options on the fingers of one big hand. "My darling brother was about to a) divorce you," one went down, "b) cut you out of his will," there went the second, "c) and have a baby with our father's widow." Gaines thought about it a second with his third finger down before shrugging. "I'm sure there's more, but that will do for now, won't it?"

Eleanor fish lipped in his direction, panic engulfing her in a physical wave that had her staggering into Albert once again. No tears this time, just a frenzied devolution into what looked to me like a crash into hysteria pending a massive meltdown.

"Mrs. Vesterville," Cherise said, drawing Eleanor's gaze, terror etched in her face, a squeaking meep all she managed in response. "Let's have a little chat, shall we?"

Albert guided her forward, whispering in her ear, Eleanor unresisting at last and I wondered if she'd finally broken. As I stepped back and away to give them room, motion in my periphery caught my attention and I noted the sight of the driver hovering near the entrance to the servant's wing, the young man's intense focus not on Eleanor at all.

Nope, Fielder Grant watched Shea while doing a terrible job of pretending not to.

Which confirmed what I'd been thinking without either of them having to say a word. Hey, my intuition was working, imagine that.

Instead of approaching the young man, I instead joined Lloyd who lingered by the front door as if uncertain of what to do from here. A gentle touch to his arm drew his attention to me, flash of an automatic smile greeting my interruption.

"How long has Fielder been working for the family?" I said it quietly, with my own smile in place, hoping to hide what I was up to, at least from the others if not from Lloyd whose gaze flickered momentarily to the lurker before he nodded once to me, expression smoothing out into genial professionalism once again.

"Six months, ma'am," he said. "Mr. Grant has been with us six months."

"And how long has Shea been with the family?" All nice and polite and nothing to see here, move along now.

Lloyd's face didn't flinch, but I caught the understanding in his eyes. "She and Mr. Reginald met ten months ago," he said. "Married nine months ago. Ma'am."

How interesting. "Thank you, Lloyd," I said. Patted his hand to give the impression I'd merely been checking in with him and then turned and walked back to the girls. Only to find they'd disappeared, along with everyone else, while Cherise spoke quietly and intently with Eleanor, Albert hovering still.

Didn't matter, since the driver had vanished back into the servant's wing. I had more than enough information I was positive now my gut reaction was correct. I didn't need a paternity test to know who the father was. Nor to check his cell phone to know it was the young driver who Shea had been talking to.

So, it was either wait for Cherise to finish and tell her what I knew or just send her a text and try to find the girls again. Decided for me when my phone buzzed and Callie's excited, all-caps message landed.

THALIA FOUND ONE. BALLROOM.

Continuing the treasure hunt hadn't been on the list of things to do at the moment, but apparently, Reginald's mystery boxes didn't care about best-laid plans.

CHAPTER SIXTEEN

I hated to interrupt her, hesitated, knowing it was important the whole family be present, only to see Cherise step back from Eleanor who spun and let Albert hold her. I took a chance and joined them, speaking softly and kindly but with firm intent.

"The girls found another box," I said. "Eleanor, are you up to—"

She looked up, nodded, all the vitriol drained from her. But it was Albert who spoke, his anger gone, dullness remaining.

"Whatever secrets Reginald still has to torment this family with," he said, "we will see this through to the end. Won't we, my darling?"

She pushed away from him as though his show of caring disgusted her, a thin sliver of the Eleanor I'd first met shining through the tattered remains of her composure. "Let's get this over with."

Gaines appeared from the corridor under the staircase, giant smirk on his face. "Shall we retire to the ballroom for another blow to the family pride?"

I let them go, lingered with Cherise who joined me, the pair of us following while I whispered to her what I'd discovered about the driver and Shea. The sheriff just nodded she'd heard me as we entered the ballroom behind Albert and Eleanor, massive space reminding me of a fairy tale, the only room so far that wasn't stained dark, white walls trimmed in gold, the crystalline marble floor sparkling in the sunlight from the towering windows at the far end. It would have taken a lot of people to make this space feel full, and rather than expansive I suddenly felt even smaller than I had before.

I suddenly couldn't wait to take my leave of Vesterville House and never come back.

Thalia held the box out as we joined her, key in her hand. "Grandpa Reginald tucked it behind one of the curtains," she said, gesturing at one of the tall views over the estate grounds on the other side, the heavy curtain drawn back to reveal the corner of the sill now empty of the prize Thalia had in her grasp. "My key doesn't fit," she said.

Gaines took it from her with a bow, grandly attempting his own, only to fail as well. When Shea tried to go next, however, Eleanor roughly pushed her aside and grabbed the black rectangle, jamming her key into the lock.

And turning it.

She threw the box to the ground, the sound of it hitting the stone floor smothered by the massive space, black skittering across white and coming to a spinning halt ten feet away. Eleanor snapped the seal before the container that held the sheet of paper she grasped in shaking hands came to a stop, jerking the page open so violently it tore at the edge, her name etched across the back side while she read the front.

"'I've known of your affair with Albert for quite some time,'" she snarled out the words, page vibrating in her grasp. "'Despite your excellent breeding and the legacy of your grandmother, Abigail, I'm most disappointed with how you turned out.'" She laughed then, a tortured sound. "You and me both, old man," she said before going on with his words in her mouth. "'I'm only glad Abigail passed before she could uncover your dishonor. Still, I was well aware Chairman, despite being my eldest, was unworthy of you.'" Eleanor drew a gasping breath, running out of air as she spit the words back at the page. "'And so, I relent. Take the key to the place we once heard her tell tales and use it to make music, my dear. Perhaps it will soothe your guilty soul.'" She cast the page aside, spinning toward the box, skidding over the marble in her heels and falling to her knees beside it, trembling hands lifting it to her, desperation in her expression as she looked around. "Where is it?"

To my surprise, it was Gaines who bent, retrieving a shining thing from the floor near his foot, everyone staring as he held it out to Eleanor. She struggled her way to her feet, still clutching the box, before snatching the key from him and turning to run from the ballroom, kicking aside her high heels as she went.

"Shall we pursue?" Gaines was already on her trail, his obvious enjoyment of his sister-in-law's torment one more mark against him, though I suppose all those years of living with this family had to add up to some kind of karma. And no matter how much I wished I could walk away, I found myself caught up in the moment with everyone else, Calliope grabbing my hand, Cherise at my side and Thalia—dear, kind and gentle Thalia—

supporting Shea in the group exodus.

"This way!" Gaines kept us appraised, at least, following his voice up the stairs to the third floor, to the left this time and more residences, waving at us at the end of the hall to hurry. We swept through the door into the sitting room of what felt like a suite long closed to fresh air, then through to the bedroom beyond.

Where Eleanor sat, a music box in her lap, at a dressing table, the mirror reflecting her slumped form while she stared down at the white lacquered rectangle in her grasp.

"I thought it was lost," she whispered. "He said all her things were packed up." Eleanor looked up at us. "He kept it, he must have. Put it back here. To torment me." She was crying again, though I doubted she knew it, gaze empty and wide open, raw and vulnerable. I took a quick glance around, imagined this could only be Abigail's room.

"How many stories did we listen to, El?" Gaines sank to a chair and crossed his long legs, hands steepling in front of him as he watched her. "You and me and Chairman when he wasn't being an arrogant snot. Donny? All sitting here, watching Abby brush her white hair, tease us about what was in the box." Wait, was that sadness in his voice? Yes, a return of sorrow, but only for Abigail, it seemed. "Time to find out what's in it, I suppose."

Eleanor stared at him a long moment before fumbling the little key and sliding it into the lock. She turned it slowly, lifting the lid with a soft breath over the moment, the faint sound of music rising from the thing. Reginald thought of everything, apparently, even wound it so it would play. While Eleanor stared down into the depths of it before lifting out a necklace.

A diamond necklace. And then a bracelet. A ring. Earrings. Finally, a sparkling tiara. All shining and rather enormously gaudy. While Gaines whistled.

"The Russian prince," he said. "She wasn't making it up."

Eleanor shook her head. "He really gave them to her. But, where's the rest?" She pulled out the divider from the box, threw it aside. "That's it?"

"You want more?" Gaines's cold, level question felt like a threat to me. "Abby's most prized possessions and you want more, Eleanor?"

She threw the music box at him though I noted she left the pile of diamonds in her lap, one hand cupping them together to protect them almost like Shea had done with her pregnant belly. "I want my part of the fortune."

Gaines climbed to his feet, hands sliding into his front pockets, big shoulders shrugging. "And now you have it. Congratulations." He turned and left the room without another word, expression almost disappointed.

Meanwhile, Eleanor seemed to have regained some of her Vestervillian attitude, surging to her feet, juggling diamond jewelry as she did. "I'll contest this will," she snarled. "These are already mine." She hugged them to her. "I want what I'm owed. I'll take this family apart if I have to!"

"Too late, Aunt Eleanor," Thalia said in the breath of an instant between Eleanor's ranting and deep inhale to carry on. "We've already done that to ourselves."

Eleanor stared at her, shaking and clearly lost. While Albert retrieved the music box and a sheet of paper at the bottom.

"My darling," he said. "Listen to this: 'Eleanor, I realize your disappointment must be crushing. That's why I'm offering you another chance.'" Her head whipped around, intensity so targeted on him it had to be uncomfortable, but he ignored her and carried on. "'If you can uncover who murdered Doncaster and Celia and finally bring that family tragedy to a close, a trust fund of $10 million will pay out the moment the killer is convicted.'"

Eleanor's soft moan said it all.

CHAPTER SEVENTEEN

I chose to exit the room after that, the heavy air choking me, Eleanor's increasingly frantic energy about the limit to what I could take. I'd been in the middle of some pretty overwhelming emotional breakdowns thanks to my professional training, but this was...

This was just. Whoa.

I hadn't noticed Shea had left, too, Cherise distracted as well, I could only guess when she'd crossed to Albert to examine the page outlining Eleanor's challenge. The pregnant widow had made good her escape and swayed her way down the hall. I followed on impulse, taking the corner, not toward the staircase, but deeper into the other wing.

Stopped when I heard a man's voice and peeked into a room to see Shea had entered.

Was speaking quietly with none other than her partner in crime, Fielder Grant. Who, to my surprise, held two boxes in his hands.

Well, now.

Shea was attempting to jam her key into one of them, hissing whisper reaching me as I approached as quietly as I could. But only after firing off a fast text to Cherise because I'd learned not to jump into a potentially dangerous situation alone, thank you.

"It doesn't fit," she said, shoulders jerking as she tried the other then stomped her foot. "It's not either of these."

Fielder's own frustration showed though he turned in a swift move, one hand raised. "There's more than one way to open a box." Aimed it at the table beside him. Prepared to what, smash it?

"I wouldn't do that if I were you." How fun, the adorable shock on their faces, and for the first time I knew why Gaines adopted amusement over anger when confronting the family. "Since the sheriff knows what you're up to."

Fielder had as many swears in his arsenal as his partner, threatening expression turning to sullen acceptance when Cherise joined us in a thudding entry that I heard long before she appeared. The only reason I chose to confront them. Because backup of the kind of epicness that was my sheriff friend?

All kinds of awesome.

"Sheriff King," I said as she came to a halt beside me, hands on her hips, looking about as impressed by their subterfuge as she was by the rest of the Vesterville's, "may I introduce Fielder Grant. Well, at least, that's the name he's using. Highly suspect, but I'm sure he'll be happy to tell you his real one once the paternity test from Chairman's reveal proves our young friend here is the father of Shea's child." I winked at her. "Oh, right, not her real name, either. But that's on you."

Cherise grunted softly. "Thanks for the intro," she said, all sarcasm, all the time.

I beamed up at her, then turned to Fielder. "I need to know," I said. "For posterity. Where did you find them?"

He handed them over to Cherise, shrugging. "The old guy didn't try too hard," he said. "One was in the movie theater under one of the front seats." They had a movie theater? Carrying on. "And the other was on his chair in the dining room." Hidden, no doubt, from casual eyes since he'd been ill and the room unused for that time. It was obvious to me Reginald's game wasn't meant to be difficult physically or mentally, at least in the discovery of the objects. No, his intent had instead been of the emotionally challenging variety.

My moment of shining success only lasted so long, Eleanor appearing at the door, still clutching her jewelry, gaze landing on the boxes in Fielder's hands, taking in his presence with Shea without flinching. If she understood the implications, she didn't say, too lost, perhaps, in her private hell, her voice now a monotone of endless agony. "Gaines found another box in the art gallery."

"Where?" Not significant, I suppose, but I needed the closure on the full set.

She didn't answer for a long time, staring soullessly at me then blinked. "Inside the helmet of plate mail he brought back from France."

"The last one, it seems," Cherise said. Gestured for the pair across the room to join and then lead us out, Eleanor stepping aside, watching them go with empty eyes. "Shall we?"

I certainly hadn't expected mere minutes later after all that came before to be standing to one side of the dining room table, three identical black boxes now laid out in a row before us, three keys remaining as the last of their owners contemplated the offering. While my mind had a thought, struggled to put pieces in place, in order, to find reason behind each placement.

Abigail Selling's photo had guarded, not Eleanor's box, but Chairman's. Why? Was Abigail standing judgment over him instead of her own granddaughter? Perhaps she'd done so when he was a child. And Albert's had been found under Reginald's bed. Was that a jab at his affair with Eleanor? Why then was hers discovered in the ballroom? None of it connected cleanly, did it? That had me even more on edge as the trio of keyholders hesitated as one while I wondered which of the boxes in front of me were found where and why they might have been left where they were.

While I had to admit there might not have been a reason at all and sighed internally at how very invested I'd become in the entire process. Reginald had been no slouch when it came to pushing people off-kilter.

Gaines finally went first with a chuckle when no one else moved, selecting the far right one. Thalia went for the center, Shea—or whoever she was—sliding the box on the left closer before trying her key.

The tension and suspense had me in knots as none of their keys worked, Gaines's wry grin as he traded with Thalia drawing a smile of her own to her lovely face. Shea nabbed Thalia's a moment later and then, with three soft expressions of satisfaction, the trio of remaining keys slid home.

And three locks clicked.

I glanced at Cherise, her agreement to allow this to wrap up on the single condition Shea was coming with her the moment it was over seemed all but forgotten. Sure, the young widow would soon find herself under arrest as her boyfriend and the father of her child (not to mention her partner in all this) had already been, led away by a deputy. At some point, this would come to an end, but not before the truth finally came out and the mystery was solved. Even Cherise seemed enraptured by the unfolding drama, and I returned my attention to the three Vestervilles as they lifted the lids of the boxes as one.

Shea's eagerness had her snatching the letter, cracking the seal and going first, though I wondered if she realized the faster she went, the quicker she'd be off to prison, but that was on her.

"'My darling Shea,'" she read, "'I am well aware you are not who you say you are.'" She faltered a little, voice trembling. "'But thanks to you, despite your deceit, I have had the most remarkable last days any man could hope for. And, since lying and cheating is a common theme in this family, you fit right in, my dear, so how could I ask you to be otherwise?'" Shea giggled just a little and for a moment I wondered if she really had cared for Reginald after all. "'While the child you bear belongs to another, my fondness for you softens my heart even as I write this. For you, for the baby you carry, I leave you one million dollars, so you never again have to lie to survive.'" She lowered the page, tears trickling down her cheeks, free hand going to her belly. "He… he knew and he still…" She looked up, turning, meeting my eyes, for some reason. "Why would he do that?"

I shrugged, answering since she seemed to be asking me. "Like he said, you brought him happiness in the end. Maybe he just wanted to take care of you."

She stared at me, more tears trickling, her first real ones, I was sure, while Gaines cracked the seal on his letter and ended Shea's moment.

"'I have always wished, my dear Gaines, we had been closer.'" His voice faltered, that beginning bluster softening into a brief moment of pause before he went on in a more normal tone. "'Your mother loved you most of all, I hope you know that. And her love, I fear, was what kept us apart. I admit to jealousy, how she doted on you, how Abigail adored you. I see now, though, the man you could have been, so much more than Chairman'." Gaines exhaled a quick, short breath. "Well, what do you know." Then went on. "'With Doncaster dead, you are the only one in the family I can trust with this most important of tasks. Watch over Thalia.'" She started at her name, turning to her uncle, her expression filled with shock and that lovely vulnerability this family had failed to crush out of her. "'Use the renewal of your trust fund that is your birthright to guide and guard your niece for she is the last Vesterville, I fear, and the best of us for her soft kindness, not despite it.'" He lowered his hands, the most remarkably tender expression crossing his face before he looked up and met Thalia's eyes. "I swear it." Gentle, those words, but agonized, piercing as the world fell away and there was only Gaines and Thalia. "I swear to you, I will always watch over you and keep you safe, Lia."

She went to him, hugged him, her head tucking under his chin, the pair embracing a long moment while the rest of us watched and hope for the Vestervilles woke in me. If he kept this promise, if Thalia was allowed to thrive, could she turn them around?

Fortunately, I'd be there to find out.

She finally released him, tiptoeing to kiss his

cheek, before sighing softly and going to her own box. It stood open, the paper inside obviously not a single sheet, though there was a top page she cracked the seal to and read it out loud, resigned but with her hope in her voice.

"'My darling Thalia, I'm sorry for the burden. But know I love you as I loved your father. Be well, my dear, and do not let it curse you as it did the rest of us.'" She set the page aside, pulling out the sheaf of papers beneath, unfolding them. "'The Last Will and Testament of Reginald Porter Krandolf Vesterville.'" She turned to Gaines, holding it out to him while Eleanor moaned deeply, a wrenching sound of an animal in her death throes. "Please, Uncle Gaines. I can't do this."

He smiled at her, tight, but confident. "Yes," he said. "You can. The old man made the right choice, kiddo. I promise you'll finally pull this family out of the dark." Gaines glanced my way, then grinned at Calliope who watched with her mouth hanging open, both hands pressed to her heart in shock. "Besides, you have a lot more help than any Vesterville has the right to ask for." He leaned in and kissed her forehead. "You got this, Lia."

As the room finally erupted.

CHAPTER EIGHTEEN

I wondered how long Gaines would let it go on, if Cherise would step in to stop the shouting, the finger-pointing. It was the worst possible torment to stand there and not rush to Thalia's side, to defend her, to shield her from this nightmare. But my mind held me still, going back to the original notion she had to stand up to them and this was the perfect time for it.

As much as that hurt me to the bottom of my soul.

"Enough." Was I surprised Thalia managed it, the very thing I'd held out for? Did so with success despite my hope I'd made the right choice. That her voice rose sufficiently to quiet them all despite her previous lack of assertion or dominance, not elevated as theirs were, but stronger, more controlled? A little, I admit it. I actually expected her to fail, not a bad thing at times, and maybe more of a lesson she needed than success. Except, that desire I'd felt earlier spawned some more of itself and grew into pride and the need to squee in delight when she did, even sprouting a few tendrils of *heck yeah* while Calliope's fists bounced against her thighs, her tight grin doing nothing to hide the vibrating adoration beaming from her face.

Gaines was right. Thalia would be just fine.

To a Vestervillian, they quieted instantly. Imagine that? My shock, I can assure you, was warranted despite all support I felt for Thalia. What possible motivation could they have had to suddenly turn, to stare at her while she did her best to remain motionless, that lovely face of hers tense with unaccustomed command. Surprise only lasted a moment, until I recognized why this shift in their attitude and action. All eyes fell to the will, and it hit me as hard as the truth she now had to face had likely struck the young woman before me.

Like it or not, Thalia held all the power, and they were, to a fault, all fully trained to comply with that power, weren't they? Whether the protesting would begin again in short order, or she'd simply slide into that place over them without contest, each and every one of the

Vesterville family realized the new reality now unfolding in front of them meant they either toed the line and took their place in the hierarchy Reginald designed long enough to bide their time to win over or depose Thalia or they could leave.

No other options remained in that frozen breath between what was and what had been. I wished it felt refreshing, like a renewal, a positive and sunny beginning for this tragic family. I knew better, as each of them visibly bowed under the inescapable inevitability of their new—and, unremarkably old—space in the grand scheme.

Let the sucking up commence.

Except, it was Gaines's turn to speak, his gaze sweeping past Albert and Eleanor, to Shea and back again. "The old man has spoken," he said, all pretense of amusement gone, harshly acerbic and without a trace of that charisma to cover his open animosity. "Each of you got exactly what you deserved. Including, dare I say, Chairman." Yikes. "Now, Sheriff King, if you'd be so kind, there are some people here I believe you need to escort off the premises."

She shrugged like she didn't take orders from him, but knew he was right. "Mrs. Vesterville?" She gestured at Eleanor who flinched and then swayed. "And Mrs.

Vesterville." This time at Shea who looked down at the letter in her hands, before clutching it to her belly and nodding.

At least if she went to prison, she had something to look forward to on the other side.

Eleanor, for her part, resisted the deputy who appeared when Cherise summoned him, twisting and turning as she was led out, near delirious gaze fixed on Thalia. "I'll find the killer for you, I promise!" Her voice echoed back to us as she was led out into the hall. "I'll find who did it and I'll make them pay, Thalia!"

Gaines's snort wasn't lost on any of us, nor was the fact it was acutely apparent her only reason for saying so had a ten-million-dollar condition attached. As for Albert, he hurried after his only remaining meal ticket, though he paused at the door to turn and speak to Thalia himself.

"I know this fortune like no one else," he said. "I can help you manage it. Thalia, don't forget. We're family." When she didn't respond, he let the awkward silence go on just a titch too long, so I was wincing when he finally slouched his way out.

Calliope clearly couldn't control her enthusiasm any longer, throwing herself past Gaines at Thalia and squealing in excitement, hugging her and bouncing in place while they both started laughing.

"This," my daughter said, breathless and wide-eyed, grin splitting her round face, "is freaking *epic*!"

Thalia exhaled a long, slow breath, soft smile of her own sad but warming up thanks to my daughter's support. She held Calliope's hand in hers as I joined them, too, Thalia only releasing her long enough to throw her arms around my neck and hug me tight. "Thank you for being here." She let me go, retrieving Calliope's hand. "Both of you." Looked up and past me. "All three of you."

Gaines's attitude had shifted once again to that jovial good nature and magnetic charm I knew now was only the façade of the man beneath. Made it easier to repel that odd attraction I'd fought all along, though not entirely. Nope. Because that man was *fine*.

So fine.

"If you don't mind," Thalia said then, "I'm feeling a bit overwhelmed. I might go upstairs and lie down for a bit. Now that everything is over."

"Of course," Gaines and I said at the exact same moment, Calliope eye-rolling at me before tugging her hand and leading her out the door. Her uncle watched them go before turning to me, sighing deeply as he met my gaze.

"I'm not entirely convinced," I said before he could speak, "you're the right person for the job. Reginald didn't have much of a selection to call on, after all." That came out a bit harsher than I'd planned, but I really needed to make sure Thalia was safe and if this was the best her grandfather had to offer when it came to watching over her, Gaines could just be sure I'd be watching him in turn, like a hawk.

Correction. A Momma Bear. Growl.

His expression darkened, but I felt nothing of a threat or pushback from him, just that same shivering intensity that I now guessed might be the core of him. "Thalia is everything to me," he said. "I loved Doncaster, looked up to him, and have adored my niece since the moment she was born. Nothing will happen to harm her, ever."

I believed him, nodded in return. And left, because there was nothing else for me to do, was there? Hey, get your mind out of the gutter. I was not going to linger and allow myself to be beguiled by Gaines Vesterville, gorgeous and delicious and complex enough to make me want to dive deep into his mind— again, you really need to wash your own out with soap—to find out what made him tick.

Instead, I found myself in the foyer,

Calliope at the door, hugging Lloyd, to my surprise.

My daughter shrugged. "She wants to sleep, told me to go. So, I go." Calliope looked sad at the dismissal. I hugged her, leading her out.

"Thalia will need us soon enough," I said. "For now, dear heavens, isn't the fresh air nice?" The sun was just setting over the edge of the estate and, for the first time in hours that felt like days, I drew a deep, deep breath.

All's well that ends well, isn't that what they say? As I pulled out of the drive past the gate and headed home, I couldn't help the soft shiver of premonition that had me rubbing goosebumps from my arm.

Why did it feel like this was far from over?

CHAPTER NINETEEN

I should have trusted my instincts, I suppose, because I had no more than pulled in my driveway, heading to my kitchen door with a weariness to my step that felt like I carried all the weight of the Vestervilles with me despite the fact I was home and out of their influence for now than another car joined mine, the red Cooper Mini as familiar as my SUV. Thalia emerged, hugging herself inside her long, wool coat, face pinched, dark circles under her eyes as she joined me at the door.

"I hope Calliope won't be mad," she whispered, voice hoarse, signs of crying in the red splotches on her cheeks and neck, the bloodshot look of her blue eyes. "I didn't mean to hurt her by sending her away. But I needed to talk to you alone."

I opened the door without another word and stepped aside for her to enter, Thalia's low cry as she bent immediately met with a soft meow. Belladonna purred deeply, rubbing her furry cheeks and forehead against Thalia's face, fresh tears dripping into the soft, white fluff. I kept my silence, knowing she'd talk when she was ready, discarding my leather jacket, taking hers while she juggled the cat, no longer in that pink dress she'd worn all day but the more casual girl I was familiar with in her baggy white t-shirt that only made her look thinner, tucked into the top of her skinny jeans. I almost offered her dinner, knowing it was metabolism and age that made her so lean, personally witness to her devouring two hamburgers and half a pizza at a time on occasion. But, before I could suggest feeding her, she sat at the kitchen peninsula with Bella snuggled close and spoke.

"I don't know what to do, Seph." She choked on every word, sobs behind them, unexpressed but waiting to come out, Thalia struggling for air, red in the face and eyes scrunched against the flow of tears. She hiccupped once, hitched a breath, wiping her cheek on the shoulder of her t-shirt as I handed her a tissue. She set Belladonna down a moment, blew her nose, dabbed at it with an apologetic air, as though she were a bother. While I sat next to her, squeezing her knee before sitting back and just waiting. Being there for her while she coughed softly past the lump in her throat and sagged. "I'm so afraid." She held the used tissue in her fist, the other hand stroking Bella's fur while the cat flipped over and offered up that most treasured of spaces for attention, silky belly exposed. "I don't want the family money. Or the curse that comes with it."

"Curse?" I couldn't help that question. "It's just money, Lia." And with the remainder of the untrustworthy (Gaines still questionable but I'd give him a pass for now) Vestervilles out of her life, surely, she'd be fine from here.

Thalia swallowed hard, jaw jumping. "All of the Vestervilles suffer in some way, Seph," she said. "You've seen just a small part of it." More than enough, thank you. "Either they lose the love of their lives long before time or can't have kids or die young themselves." She bowed her head over Belladonna, kissing her forehead, the cat batting at her long, blonde hair escaping from the confines of the ponytail she'd adopted. When Thalia met my eyes, I almost hugged her, held off, from the depth of fear in her, the surety she was doomed, so clearly written in her. "The whole family whispers about it. That the money and the house are cursed."

"Sweetie, I know you've had a rough go." Wow, Persephone, that was truly an epic understatement. I grasped her hand, tissue and all, and made her focus on me until she sighed, nodded. "I knew things were hard for you, but I had no idea. Not until now. And I promise you, I'm going to make sure you have all the support you need."

"You always have, Seph," Thalia said, faint smile rising. "You and Callie and Trent have always been there for me." Right. I kept forgetting while I was like a mom to her, my ex had played the surrogate father role more than once. Hopefully, he had continued. "I'm sorry, I didn't mean to make you feel guilty. This isn't your problem."

She tried to rise but, at that same moment, I tugged on her to stay while Bella let out a murmured chirp and batted her arm. Thalia laughed a little, going back to stroking the cat's belly while I released her hand and shrugged.

"Listen, kid," I said, "you're a part of my family, have been since you and Callie were six and she punched that boy in the nose for being mean to you." Thalia giggled, nodded, her sadness and fear fading a little. "I've watched you grow, you and Callie together, and I know you can do this." Okay, maybe I was worried. Just a little. Like, more than a little. But I wasn't telling her that, not when she was obviously looking for some reason to trust herself. Thalia's self-doubt rose, crested in a deep breath, fell away as I went on. "Whatever happens, curse or just bad luck or whatever other reason for your family's troubles, it doesn't have to go on. It can end. With you."

She squared her shoulders a little, gaze brightening, fear faded at last. "I didn't mean to come here and freak out on you."

"You come here anytime," I said, "and freak out on me," I pointed at Belladonna who let out another chirp, "and her as often as you want. Okay?" She gave me the tiniest nod. "Now, tell me. What do you want to do?"

Thalia gaped at me, eyes wide, before inhaling a short breath. "What do you mean?"

"I mean," I said, all humor gone, "what do you want to do with the fortune? Just because he gave it to you, doesn't mean you have to keep it. Or the house. Thalia, I think you're afraid because he trapped you in this. But he didn't. Your grandfather forgot you have free will and those who love you only want your happiness. There are ways and opportunities to step away from this, you know. Say the word."

She clearly hadn't thought of that. "Like

what?" Breathless, anticipating. Hopeful.

Awesome.

"Give it all away," I said. "Pick a charity, a bunch of them. Sell the house. Tear it down. Do whatever you want. It's yours." I let that sink into her for a minute while she leaned away from me, aghast until the truth absorbed, and she laughed.

And laughed. Near hysteria, clutching her ribs, giggling and then openly laughing while more tears streamed down her face. Caught her breath, leaned toward me with one hand on my shoulder. "Grandpa Reginald would be *furious*."

I grinned back. "Grandpa Reginald now resides in an urn."

She settled somewhat, still smiling. "Eleanor wouldn't stand for it."

"Eleanor doesn't have a say." It still hadn't gotten through to her completely, it seemed, but I was stubborn and persistent, and I was not letting this young woman I adored suffer if she chose otherwise.

"Uncle Gaines would be disappointed." Thalia hesitated at that, guilt rising on her face.

"Your Uncle Gaines would find it hilarious and cheer you on," I said. "And you know it."

She snorted, wry smile following. "He would." Her hand went back to Belladonna who head-butted her fingers, green eyes closing in dreamy joy. "I don't want to live in the house alone."

There was the crux, perhaps. "So don't," I said. "Don't live in it, or do live in it, but make your own choices. Be Thalia, not a Vesterville."

She flashed me a smile. "Thank you, Seph," she said. Before yawning, a massive, jaw-popping yawn that caught her by surprise. She giggled, shook her head. "Sorry, I really am tired. I should go."

"I have a better idea." I lifted Belladonna into her arms and then drew her to her feet, guiding her toward the stairs. "Go lie down. You know where Callie's room is. Have a nap. I'll make dinner. We'll call her in a bit, and we'll all talk this out. Okay?"

Thalia leaned into me and kissed my cheek. "Thanks, Mom." She hadn't called me that since she was little, caught me by surprise, tears rising in my eyes as I waved her off.

Watched her climb the stairs with my cat in her arms and the whole weight of the family on her shoulders, not moving until the sound of Calliope's door opening and closing told me Thalia was safe and sound.

Turned in the dark hallway to find my phone in my purse, most of the house lights still out. And felt it buzz in my hand.

Read the message, frowning at the text

from a number I didn't recognize.

A single image. I tapped it, expanded it. Read the cleaning services menu. While my chest constricted. *Suit*, it listed. *$25k. Dress, $25k. Pink skirt, $15k. Blue pants, $15k.* On and on, with group pricing for various items, all of which, I was very sure, had nothing to do with cleaning.

This was a hired hit list.

May we ask who referred you? That message popped up underneath while I stared in horror at the menu.

I'm messaging for Chairman Vesterville, I sent back, thinking about the black business card, the implications of this whole conversation. *He ordered a suit and a dress several years ago.* Please, let me be wrong, but I knew I was right.

Is this about the pink skirt from his original order? Pink skirt. Oh no. Thalia was supposed to be with her parents the weekend they died but stayed in Wallace because she had the flu. Except she really just didn't want to go. I knew she carried that guilt with her still. *Thank Mr. Vesterville for his understanding and that the order remains open if he wants to renew it.*

I didn't respond, stomach churning, sick dread buckling my knees and sending me to sit on the bench by the door, heart pounding. Eleanor was going to be furious.

I just found out who killed Doncaster and Celia Vesterville which meant not only was her husband a murderer who'd been murdered, but she was out ten million dollars.

CHAPTER TWENTY

I forwarded the texts to Cherise, knowing she'd be angry with me for taking such a risk while firing off a final message to the service.

We'll be in touch.

We appreciate your business.

So professional.

It had me heading for my office, for my computer and research into the Vesterville family, the curse Thalia mentioned, Chairman and Doncaster and the whole mess that was their spiraling bloodline into disaster despite their old hoard of money. Or, perhaps, because of it.

Came across a photo that had me pausing to read, a newspaper article about Abigail Selling, still lovely but in her 80s when the image was taken, handsome young Chairman at her side, Doncaster beside him, and who could only be Gaines, barely eighteen, sitting next to her where she smiled from her wheelchair. Some sort of charity event for WWII veterans. Quotes from her about the war, from Doncaster and Chairman and one in particular from Gaines that caught my attention. *Abby is so inspiring,* he'd told the reporter. *We're so proud of all she accomplished, she's like part of the family. Her stories make me want to be a spy like her someday.*

I left my office, thinking about it, heading for the kitchen. Paused at the stairs, looking up to where Thalia slept, lost in the possibilities. What *had* Gaines been up to? He'd been out of touch with the family a long time, didn't live in Wallace or at the estate. Hadn't for ages, in fact. I pulled out my phone, did a quick search. Caught my breath at what I found.

Realized the truth.

Dialed Cherise.

Caught the scent I knew so well just as a big hand reached around me, took my phone, his breath on my cheek, his voice low in my ear.

"It's not what you think," Gaines said. "Let's have a talk, clever and beautiful Persephone Pringle, before you do something we'll both regret."

Never mind I was already regretting a lot of

things, like not locking the door though I doubt it would have kept someone like him out. And did the only thing I could do.

"Want a drink?" I headed for the kitchen like my life wasn't in danger because even if he didn't say yes? I needed gin for this.

Before I accused him of murdering his own brother, that was.

You know, the only reason I managed to remain so calm was the fact I was attracted to him still. Funny, right? One would think I'd have gone blubbery sob fest on his butt. Instead, I held onto the fact he was so handsome and wasn't threatening me, not really, that he simply set my phone on the counter out of my reach before sitting with that sexy smile of his, nodding when I opened the cupboard door and shook the gin bottle in his direction.

The ice might have rattled a bit more loudly than usual because my hands were shaking but I managed to pour both drinks without spilling and even circled to sit next to him where Thalia had just been, sliding his toward him—water, no cranberry, as requested—while I took a long drink of mine and wished I'd made it a triple.

Heck, upended the bottle into my mouth.

Steady, woman. Steady.

He tasted the drink, set it aside. "I wasn't sure what to expect from you," he said, arms crossing over that broad chest, still in the white dress shirt but with a more casual jacket over it now rather than the dress one he'd worn. Jeans hugged his long legs, cowboy boots on his feet, more rugged than polished now, but no less stunningly delicious. "I heard great things, from Doncaster and Celia over the years. Saw you and your FBI husband at the funeral. You seemed genuine and, from what I researched, you're respected so I trusted you had Thalia's back while I did what I had to do."

"Be a spy, you mean," I said.

He chuckled, shrugged, blue eyes sparkling. "I didn't even need the alert you'd pinged my old service records to know you'd figured that much out." Another sip, a long, speculative study of my person while I fought off the shakes and took another long drink of my own, ice tapping my upper lip when I drained it. Didn't trust myself enough to stand and pour another, nor that being tipsy was a good thing after all at a time like this. While Gaines finally went on.

"You've uncovered my secret," he said. "And now I'm not sure what to do about it."

"I'm surprised no one else has," I said, going for boldness because otherwise I'd be crying and begging him not to kill me. "Did they really buy the fact you were kicked out of the Air Force?"

He laughed at that. "Of course, they did," he said. "None of them understood why I joined in the first place when I had all that family money and years of lecherous, wasteful debauchery at the family fortune to look forward to."

"I take it the dishonorable discharge was a front," I said.

He shrugged, sipped. Stared into his drink a moment. "We Vestervillians have such a flare for the dramatic, don't you agree?" Gaines set the glass aside, though he didn't release it, swirling it in the puddle of condensation left behind. "It was her idea." Abigail, had to be. "She had old contacts, suggested I would be better suited to more... clandestine pursuits and that I was being wasted as a trust-fund kid. She was right."

"So, you joined the CIA or something?" I was grasping for acronyms, clearly.

Gaines's blue eyes flickered to mine from the glass. "Or something. I'm a little more international than our government can manage." Since the CIA was literally outside the States, I had to believe he was recruited by an organization I'd never heard of and would likely be killed if I ever found out. "The point being, I'd decided long ago to displace myself from the events of the family's spiral into their own filth. Until." He clinked his ice. "Another?"

I had no idea how I managed it, but I did, though mine was weak, barely a half ounce, though when I sat, I found I'd stopped shaking at least, the warmth of the alcohol steadying my insides.

He took another sip, saluting me before continuing. "I was on mission," he said, sadness in his voice, on his handsome face, "when I heard Doncaster and Celia had been murdered. Believe me, Seph, I will regret that for the rest of my life." His jaw clenched then released. "I came home as quickly as possible, but it was too late. They were gone. All I could do was ensure Thalia was safe before I went hunting."

"How?" I needed to keep my mouth shut. But that question blurted out anyway.

"Our family's butler wasn't chosen by chance," he said with a wink. "I told you the name of the second man in the photo, the young one behind Abigail, but you didn't put it together, did you?" I shook my head. "Well, his son took over, but only after a stint working with the likes of me." Oh, my. "I suppose you'd never have reason to ask Lloyd's last name. It's Mitchem, in case you missed it."

Well now. This whole day was full of surprises.

"You left," I said. "For what? To find your brother's killers?" Of course.

He nodded. "I found the same cleaning service you did," he said as though it were a small thing, inconsequential. "Cancelled the order for Thalia's life. Knew immediately it was Chairman who ordered their deaths and why."

"Money," I said.

"The family fortune." Gaines spoke those words like they themselves were a curse. "As though that tainted money was worth more than all the lives it ended before time." He sighed gently, finished his second drink, again setting it aside, though this time he let the glass go, hands on his thighs, eyes locked on me. "I knew Chairman had to die for what he'd done, but I needed it to be fitting, his end. Classically Vestervillian. And in the most crushing way possible." There was the darkness, the heartless and empty man inside, free of compassion, empathy, driven by vengeance.

Was it wrong it made him hotter? Yes, Persephone. Yes, so wrong.

"The trouble was, I was called away to… handle a problem for my employers." I would never know the details of that simple sentence, but my mind went wild with endless possibilities, only dragged back from the brink of Hollywoodesque fantasy by his continuing story. "I only recently returned, in time to discover Father was dying and that he'd married that... young woman." There was a ringing endorsement. Gaines's lopsided grin spoke volumes. "I took the opportunity to do some digging while Father deteriorated, uncovered Chairman's plan to cut all of us out of the fortune after Father's death. Decided it was the perfect opportunity to have some fun. And told Father everything."

Oh.

Oh, no.

"You're the source of the boxes and keys," I said. While I realized then of course the old man had to have had assistance in his plan. He'd been ill, right? It made total sense now, thinking about it. An accomplice, and more than that.

He laughed out loud, head back, full of the enjoyment of the reveal, something he surely never expected to have the chance to do and was clearly loving. When Gaines fell quiet again, he bowed his head to me. "Far more clever than beautiful, and that's saying something."

Enough with the hormone prodding, Gaines. "The placement," I said. "Did they mean anything?"

He shook his head, delight in his eyes. "Not a blessed thing," he said. "Though I know you wanted them to. That was part of the fun, Seph."

So, my last-minute guesswork had been a waste of time. Lovely. Not that it mattered now, but for some reason my brain wanted things to make sense and it was clear to me now that messing with everyone involved had been part of the agenda.

"Father agreed to it with very little convincing," he said. "Even he'd had enough, you see, especially when I told him what Chairman had done. He even volunteered to give everything to Thalia before I suggested it." Gaines leaned forward, one elbow on the counter. "All that was left was to make sure Chairman wasn't part of the final show."

"Why bother with the boxes?" So many questions and he didn't seem opposed to answering. Probably because he was going to kill me anyway, so for him it was a win-win, right?

"Come now, I had to have *some* fun." He leaned his face in his hand, smile so sweet, almost innocent. "And what fun it was, Seph.

Seeing their little faces fall, hearing their wails of anguish and knowing they suffered in the end. All but Shea." He shrugged. "I didn't care really what Reginald wanted when it came to her, so she can keep the money. When she gets out of prison."

"You dosed the almonds with Abigail's cyanide," I said.

"Easy enough to dissolve the crystals in water," he said, "soak the almonds. Since the taste and smell wouldn't seem off, it was the perfect choice."

Sounded like he might have known from experience, but that was a moot point at the moment. "Then, what? Hoped no one else would eat them? What if someone had?"

He shook his head, one finger tapping my knee, sly smile emerging. "Ah, but that was the trick, wasn't it? Knowing my brother as well as I did. Getting him all worked up while I held something in my hands, showed interest in that thing. Worked on Chairman every time, don't you know, the easiest way to manipulate my brother."

"You knew he'd take them from you." I almost shook my head in admiration, held still with a vast amount of willpower. "You used Eleanor's property, had Shea handle the bowl then used Chairman's nasty bullying greed against him."

Gaines sat back again, arms spread wide. "See? Fun, right?"

"But why frame Eleanor?" Did she have something to do with hiring the cleaning service? Was she complicit?

Turned out his reasoning was much more personal than that. "She abandoned Abigail in her last hours," he said, with enough vicious hatred in that single statement he'd been holding onto the need to find a way to make her pay for a very long time. "Discarded her legacy, was going to throw it all away. That's why I took the music box." So, it had been Gaines, not his father. Had likely known about the contents all along.

"Why give it to Eleanor?" It seemed a counterintuitive move. If he hated her, why give her that most valuable of Abigail's treasures?

Those lovely lips pursed into a line, his slow blink of pleasure unexpected. "I giveth," he said, "and I taketh away."

She'd never get to enjoy them, would she, if he got his way? She'd be in prison for the rest of her life and the only thing she'd wanted of her grandmother's beyond her reach.

The presented depth of his cruelty had me shuddering.

Gaines didn't seem to notice, carried on. "I talked Father into keeping Abigail's things, but they weren't Eleanor's any longer."

"They were yours," I said. "You dusted her uniform, the painting of her."

"I had to do something to hide my tracks," he said. "And it had been too long since I visited. The sight of so much neglect…" Gaines had a heart, it seemed, but guided by its own rules and sense of right and wrong skewed not just by the family, but by years working in clandestine operations. Maybe being born a Vesterville made him the perfect choice to be a spy, but they both left their mark and I struggled not to feel compassion.

He was going to kill me, I was positive of it. So why did empathy win?

"You must be very good at what you do," I said.

He paused then, his face falling into quiet nothingness. "I'm not the only one." He cocked his head to one side. "Though, I'm aware of the techniques you're using to keep me talking. But be sure, Seph. I'm only telling you because I want you to know. Because of Thalia." His expression, so varied, shifted again, this time to thoughtful regret. "I'll do everything in my power to protect her from now on. It's time to take responsibility, to plant my own roots, I suppose. Which means I'm not going anywhere." Giving up the craft for Thalia? "I failed her father, but I won't fail her."

"Abigail would approve," I said, making a mental leap. Because I was right and wrong about him. He was the most trustworthy man I'd ever met. He just had a particular code of ethics, of honor, seeded by the woman he admired.

He flashed a grin. "You would have loved her," he said. "And she would have adored you. That's why I'm so sorry about how this has to end."

Here we were at last. "Killing me won't protect her," I said, impressed with how steady my voice was. "You want to hurt her further, murder me. You'll shatter her and you know it."

Gaines hesitated, shook his head. "She has me now," he said. "She'll survive. Turn to me more than ever. I'll make sure she endures. That lovely daughter of yours will help, I imagine."

He could just stay away from Calliope. A shock of heated anger drove me forward, Momma Bear roaring in my head. "You touch my daughter," I snarled, "and you won't have to worry about a Vestervillian curse, Gaines. I'll come back from the grave and kill you myself."

His surprise at my reaction had him blinking, then laughing while I felt my entire being tense. I amused him. How lovely.

We'd just see about that.

"If I put the pieces together," I said then, "so will Cherise King."

"Your sheriff won't have a chance," he said. "I've covered the tracks you discovered. She'll find nothing, so thank you for unearthing the past I'd forgotten to cleanse." He tapped the side of his empty glass. "I'll give you time for one more if you like? Trust me, this is the last thing I want. In fact, you intrigue me so much, I'd love the chance to get to know you better, Seph. But Thalia has to come first and that means I have no choice."

"You do," Thalia said when she emerged from the dark hallway to the light of the kitchen, staring at her uncle who had stiffened at her successfully stealthy approach. "Or you'd better come up with one, Uncle Gaines. Because if you kill Persephone, you'd better be prepared to murder me, too."

CHAPTER TWENTY-ONE

Gaines didn't respond right away, the tall, willowy young woman coming to stand next to me rather than her own uncle, arms around me, cheek leaning against the top of my head, her physical shielding of me either intentional or just a visceral response to the threat he posed to me. Whatever her intent, she'd drawn her line in the sand that was Gaines's decision to clean up behind him with that simple act.

I watched him sit there and watch us back without moving or speaking, observing the connection I felt with Thalia while, as the silence stretched out, his expression shifted from that stolid grimness to a subtler grief she'd chosen me over him.

Was he really surprised? He shouldn't have been. Of all people, Gaines Vesterville knew the inadequacy of blood ties over love. Then again, maybe he didn't and that was the saddest part of all.

A kitty grunt preceded the soft landing of Belladonna on the surface of the counter, her sudden appearance shattering the long and aching stillness with her comical and yet weighty presence. Fearless and unknowing, or uncaring more than likely the case, she sniffed his drink, sampling the moisture from the side of the glass, before sitting with her giant tail wrapped around her paws, observing him in feline judgment as though deciding if his soul was worthy of saving or not.

Gaines reached out and, in a bit of panic, I almost cried out. What if he hurt Bella to hurt me, threatened to since Thalia was now out of his reach? Instead, he stroked her fur with a tender expression while she did nothing, a statue of examination and perception he finally sighed over before returning his attention to us.

"Your cat finds me wanting," he said.

"My cat is an excellent judge of character," I said. Wished she'd stop staring at him like that, sill not trusting him to refrain from harming her or threatening her to demand my compliance.

I misread him, knew it when I caught his

regret and recognition of my anxiety, how his hand dropped away from her, both spreading out in front of him in a gesture of peace to prove to me he was no threat to my cat.

Nope, just to me. Well, if it was Belladonna or Persephone on the block, I was the one who'd earned it.

Gaines's soft smile was sad enough it rang true when he spoke next. "What am I going to do with you two, then?" His voice vibrated, an ache to his words, pleading on his face that felt authentic despite the fact he fought an internal battle between his safety and that of his niece.

"Nothing, uncle," Thalia said, firm and with that newfound conviction she'd discovered only this evening when the full weight of the Vesterville fortune landed in her delicate lap. "I love you. I don't care what you did, why you did it. You're my hero and you always will be." I didn't mention how messed up that was, how he'd murdered for her and that made him a criminal, kind of the exact opposite, right? Wait, had she missed part of the conversation, then? Or did she know everything? "Thank you for avenging my parents." Okay, she had heard it all, free of tears, so either she'd run out of them, or she was over it for now. In shock, perhaps? Or just finding herself. Far more a Vesterville than was good for her. Whatever the case, when he nodded slowly in acknowledgment, she went on in that same soft but firm voice. "I understand why you killed Uncle Chairman. So does Seph, right, Seph?" I caught myself nodding back, despite myself. Cherise would kick my butt, but yes, while I could never condone, I understood. "And why you talked Grandpa Reginald into giving me the fortune."

"No one else is worthy of it," he said.

"Not even you?" She straightened up, still with one arm draped around my shoulders while Gaines laughed.

"Least of all me, sweet girl," he said. "After all that I've done. And not just to the family." What *had* he done? Where had he been all these years? Now I really wanted to know. Since he wasn't going to kill me or anything anymore. Hopefully. Curiosity could replace anxiety, while I wondered if there was something wrong with me I fell into it so easily instead of focusing on finding a way to make him face justice for killing his own brother.

Funny how quickly things could shift from the deadly to the fascinating.

Thalia looked down at me, then back to him. "So, we're agreed? You won't hurt Seph, and we'll keep your secrets—all of them," she had to add that caveat so I couldn't selectively reveal one or two Cherise might need to solve Chairman's murder,"—and I'll figure out what I'm going to do with the house and the money and everything."

He hesitated before sighing. "Thalia," he said, "if she lives… I can't stay." He shook his head when she tried to protest. "I realize you can be trusted with certain things," he said to me. "But I have a number of… acquaintances who, if they ever found out you knew about me, could make my life… uncomfortable."

"Of course, you have to go," I said then, leaping to an understanding I don't think he'd reached himself yet or failed to allow himself to accept. "Gaines, you can't just come home and pretend you're not who you are." Was that really his plan, honestly? What was he thinking? My fear had returned, but this time not for my own personal protection. "Those same acquaintances you mentioned wouldn't think twice about using Thalia against you, would they?" I found my hands were shaking, had to clasp them tightly together. "I won't let you put her life in danger because of your past. Of all people, you have to understand what you're suggesting will never work out. You made the choice to be who you are a long time ago. Don't make Thalia pay for that choice just because you're feeling some misguided guilt.

Imagine how guilty you'll feel when one of your enemies finds you and takes it out on your niece."

He'd stilled, gone rigid, glaring at me as I pushed relentlessly through the scenario I'd laid out. Kill me or not for speaking up, I had to get through to him. Even as I shivered inside at the resistance he offered, the menace and intimidation that dominated the space between us when I didn't let him off the hook.

Gaines had to face the truth he knew in his heart already. Or one day Thalia—and my daughter, you better believe Calliope's future so tied to this entire mess, was on my mind— might pay for who he'd become.

"Wait, no." Thalia let me go, stepping back from both of us, face contorting as the tears finally came. "You promised you'd stay. You can't leave. You have to help me."

Gaines didn't look at her, still staring at me with all his hurt and rebellion being smothered by compliance. Before he turned to her, hands outstretched. She ran to him, crossing the two steps it took to hug him tight while he sighed into her hair.

"Seph's right, kiddo," he whispered. "The only way I can keep you safe is to leave you." He pushed her gently away. "I would do anything for you. Including this."

She sobbed into her hands while he looked up as he stood, handing her off to me, blue eyes full of his own tears I was positive were real.

"Take care of her," he said. And left, long strides carrying him to the door and out again, Thalia far too late as she realized he'd gone, running after him but stopping when I chased her, both hands pressed to her mouth while she wept at the sight of the empty driveway, her remarkable uncle already disappeared into the night.

I held her as she cried, Thalia begging me in whispers not to tell anyone, not to go after him. She needn't have worried. While I knew the law enforcement people in my life would be furious if they found out, who was I to go up against an international spy, anyway?

As long as Thalia was safe, all was right in the world.

I guided her inside at last, closing the door behind us, wishing Gaines well and knowing it wasn't the last I'd be seeing of him.

CHAPTER TWENTY-TWO

The sound of giggling had me grinning, Cherise chuckling over her drink, three girls whispering when they were supposed to be studying calculus the most beautiful sound in the world.

"I don't know why I bother thinking Layla will get any work done when she's here." The sheriff's oldest daughter might have been a year behind Calliope and Thalia, but the trio fit together pretty seamlessly and as far as I was concerned friendship trumped math every day of the week.

Yes, I was biased because I sucked at math. Happy?

"Bella!" That was followed by a burst of laughter. I leaned across the counter, spotted the big cat sprawling in the middle of Thalia's papers, somehow managing to plant her tail in Layla's while her front paws pushed Calliope's off the table. The three instantly dropped what they were doing and started petting her, purrs loud enough to be heard in the kitchen.

"Another?" I topped up the sheriff's drink and then my own, the scent of lasagna she'd brought reheating in the oven heavenly, though I'd managed a batch of keto-friendly buns just to placate my need to minimize the carb load I was about to consume. Oh, the lies I told my hips and thighs when pasta was available.

"You realize this is your third successful murder investigation," Cherise said over her glass of gin while discomfort at lying to her had me turning around to grab the cranberry so she wouldn't see me wince. "Eleanor's not confessing, but with the evidence in hand, it's a slam-dunk." She set her glass down, eyeing me sideways then. "Something you want to tell me?"

"Nope," I said, the promise I made intact though Eleanor's prison sentence would haunt me. "I hear that she's not collecting on her inheritance despite the fact there's evidence Chairman had Thalia's parents killed." Don't ask me how he managed it before he left, but Gaines made certain that particular bit of truth came to the sheriff's attention shortly after our conversation.

"I don't think Eleanor's going to be in a position to worry about her inheritance for a long time," Cherise saluted me. "Not only did the chemical test come back positive, that the cyanide her grandmother left her was a perfect match to the poison on the almonds, there's a case to be made she knew about her husband's plan to have Doncaster and Celia killed." If she had, I'd feel better about letting her go to prison for Gaines's actions. No way of knowing, really, while that black business card with the deeply etched phone number on the back sat in my office drawer and glared at me every time I opened it. "I'm sure she'll take a plea."

Since that was the argument keeping my sanity intact—that Eleanor was in on it so she deserved to be punished, right?—I fought off yet another flinch and pushed on before my burning culpability and remorse could put an end to my silence, a silence I had to keep to protect Thalia and would until the bitter end.

"So much for Gaines Vesterville fulfilling his father's wishes, though." Cherise had lowered her voice, glancing around the corner herself before leaning closer. "Poor Thalia. I heard he skipped town and took his inheritance with him."

I shrugged at that, fetching down plates. My, how much there was to do to prepare for dinner and not meet Cherise in the eye in the most uncomfortable way possible. "She'll be fine," I said. "She has us and that's more than enough." I changed the subject before I could blurt something that would lead Cherise down a road I didn't want her to walk. "I hear Albert is trying to contest the will."

The sheriff groaned softly. "Like he'll get anywhere. There's nothing to contest. I think he's still trying to impress Eleanor. Like she might get off. Poor deluded sucker."

"And Shea?" That's it, Persephone. Keep her distracted.

"You mean Madison Richards? Oh, and that brilliant brick she's in love with? Used his own real name." She shook her head. "Not the brightest bulb in the box, but that's love for you. At least she'll have something to come home to when her time is up."

"She didn't do anything wrong," I said.

"Not in this instance," she said. "But the pair are wanted for fraud and a few other minor infractions. The FBI is handling it, actually. Trent took it on because they crossed state lines with their activities." Well, good for him. My ex was a great agent. As long as he kept the two of them far away from Thalia.

The girls emerged from the dining room, Thalia carrying Belladonna, Layla grabbing a pile of napkins before kissing her mother's dark cheek with her full lips, amazing shining corkscrew curls wider than her narrow shoulders likely what Cherise's would look like if she didn't nearly shave her own head, Calliope circled to join me and help with cutlery. The more I focused on it as my chattering and happy guests made themselves useful and set the table now free of calculus homework, the more certain I was of the feelings shared between my daughter and the young woman I thought of as close enough. From subtle looks to brief hand touches and small, secret smiles, it was so obvious to me they had deeper feelings than friendship I just wished they'd come out with it and tell me.

Was sure they planned to when, dinner over and Cherise and Layla gone, Calliope and Thalia joined me in the kitchen to help me load the dishwasher.

"Mom," my daughter said, breathless excitement impossible for her to hide. "Thalia and I have something to tell you."

I smiled at them both, stopped what I was doing, gave them my full attention. It wasn't every day your child came out to you, after all.

"You know how Lia doesn't want to live

alone in Vesterville house?" I nodded, waited as Calliope looked to Thalia and Thalia finished.

"I asked Callie to move in with me," she said.

"And I said yes!"

I waited for the full reveal, the two of them beaming at me, their smiles fading when I didn't speak. But the real story never came and, finally realizing it wasn't going to, I managed some enthusiasm while being disappointed. Hugged them both, that same disappointment now mixing with worry.

Not just for Thalia. But my daughter now, too. Living in that house with the potential for Gaines and his choice of employment becoming a problem at some point, never mind the Vesterville family curse I really didn't believe in.

Right?

Yeah. Right. Okay then.

Whatever happened, I'd be here for them both.

I might not have been an international spy of mystery and intrigue, but I had other tools in my arsenal I planned to pull out at every opportunity to ensure my girls were safe and knew I had their backs.

Momma Bear at the ready.

Looking for more from Persephone Pringle?
You're in luck! Book three, *Coffee, Tea or
Murder Me*, is available right now!

ABOUT THE AUTHOR

Everything you need to know about me is in this one statement: I've wanted to be a writer since I was a little girl, and now I'm doing it. How cool is that, being able to follow your dream and make it reality? I've tried everything from university to college, graduating the second with a journalism diploma (I sucked at telling real stories), am an enthusiastic member of an all-girl improv troupe (if you've never tried it, I highly recommend making things up as you go along as often as possible) and I get to teach and perform with an amazing group of women I adore. I've even been in a Celtic girl band (some of our stuff is on YouTube!) and was an independent filmmaker. You can check out the whole Lovely Witches Club series for free at:

https://lovelywitchesclub.com.

My life has been one creative thing after another—all leading me here, to writing books for a living.

Now with multiple series in happy publication, I live on beautiful and magical Prince Edward Island (I know you've heard of Anne of Green Gables) with my multitude of pets.

I love-love-love hearing from you! You can reach me (and I promise I'll message back) at https://patti@pattilarsen.com/home. And if you're eager for your next dose of Patti Larsen books (usually about one release a month) come join my mailing list! All the best up and coming, giveaways, contests and, of course, my observations on the world (aren't you just dying to know what I think about everything?) all in one place:

https://bit.ly/PattiLarsenEmail.

Last—but not least!—I hope you enjoyed what you read! Your happiness is my happiness. And I'd love to hear just what you thought. A review where you found this book would mean the world to me—reviews feed writers more than you will ever know. So, loved it (or not so much), your honest review would make my day. Thank you!